KT-439-350

ROBIN JARVIS

With illustrations by the author

EGMONT

EGMONT

We bring stories to life

First published in Great Britain in 2016
by Egmont UK Limited
The Yellow Building, 1 Nicholas Road, London W11 4AN

PB ISBN 978 1 4052 8023 5
HB ISBN 978 1 4052 8508 7

www.egmont.co.uk

A CIP catalogue record for this title is available from the British Library

Typeset by Avon DataSet Ltd, Bidford on Avon, Warwickshire
Printed and bound in Great Britain by the CPI Group

The cold dark sea is watching,
and vengeance boils the tide.
A final doom is surging,
to drown old Whitby's pride.

Whitby

1. Lil's House
2. Thistlewood's Amusements
3. Cherry's Cottage
4. Whitby Gothic
5. The Abbey
6. Church and Graveyard
7. Whalebone Arch
8. Lighthouses
9. Fish Pier
10. The 199 Steps

Beach

River Esk

Khyber Pass

Pier Road

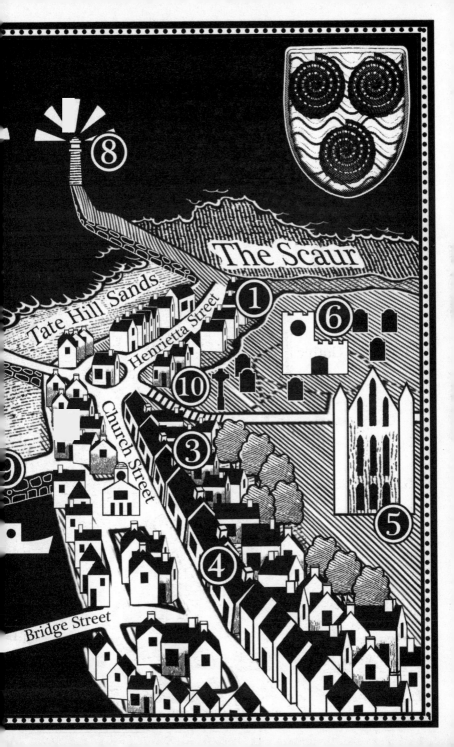

The Scaur

Tate Hill Sands

Henrietta Street

Church Street

Bridge Street

① ⑥ ⑩ ③ ⑤ ④ ⑧

ATTACK

The din of Verne Thistlewood's frantic pursuit echoed down the narrow lanes of the East Cliff. His feet thudded over the cobbles and his heart was hammering in his chest, but all he could hear were the taunts and threats of the three older girls behind him. Verne wasn't a fast runner. They were almost upon him, and they were vicious.

Bursting from the lane, he dashed into the open area of Market Place and spun round desperately. Where could he go? Which was the safest way?

The girls came shrieking after him. Before he could dodge them, they spread out, cutting off his best chances of escape,

'Get him!' Tracy Evans yelled as they closed in.

Verne pelted into the only way left, a slim passageway leading on to Fish Pier. This spur of stone jutted into the river. He had hoped he could jump down on to the shore, dart along the sand, then run up

1

the nearest set of steps. But the tide was high and the sand was deep beneath rough, foam-marbled waves that smacked the harbour wall. Verne was trapped.

Fearfully, he turned to face Tracy and her two cronies, Bev and Angie. Their faces were ugly and alive with aggression.

'What you run off for, Flimsy?' Tracy asked. 'I only wanted a chat.'

Verne edged further along the pier.

'Look at him!' Bev cried with a snort. 'He's shivering – ha!'

'You scared, Flimsy?' Tracy demanded, stalking closer.

'Don't call me that,' the boy told her.

Tracy's hand flashed out and grabbed the scarf round his neck. Twisting it in her fist until he choked, she shook him from side to side like a rag doll then shoved him backwards. The boy crashed on to the cold, wet stone. The girls laughed and Bev took out her phone to film it.

'Now you listen,' Tracy snarled, leaning over him and squeezing his thin face in her strong fingers. 'If my boyfriend loses any more money in your family's rip-off arcade, I'll come looking for you. You got that? How's he supposed to take me out and buy me stuff without any dosh? I'm not cheap.'

'Could've fooled me,' Verne said bravely as he tried to get up.

Tracy shoved him down again and slapped him hard.

'Ha!' Bev squealed. 'He's crying!'

Tracy stood back so that Bev could get a clear view on her phone. Then, with a curling lip, she told Angie, 'Take his shoes off and lob them in the river.'

Angie grabbed at Verne's flailing legs, while Tracy dragged the rucksack from his arms and swung it round to cast it into the waves.

'Leave him alone!' a new voice demanded. 'And put the bag down.'

Verne's attackers whipped round and saw a younger girl approaching along the pier. The black cloak she wore over her school uniform was flapping madly in the wind and a vivid streak of blue in her hair whipped above her brow.

'What do you want, Wilson?' Tracy snapped.

'I've already told you. Don't make me say it twice.'

'Get lost!'

Bev and Angie looked at the new girl uneasily. Lil Wilson was a weirdo. Even though they were older than her, she gave them the creeps.

'Leave it, Trace,' Bev said, returning the phone to her pocket.

Tracy bared her teeth. 'She don't scare me!' she said.

'You sure about that?' Lil asked. 'Because I'd be really worried if I was you.'

'Why's that then?'

'You know what my mum and dad are.'

'Mental!'

'Witches,' Lil corrected.

She raised her hand and the many silver rings that adorned her fingers glinted as she made a mysterious sign in the air.

'What's she doin'?' Angie asked nervously.

Lil took a deep breath and half closed her eyes.

'Selvedge aran intarsia shibori sirdar attente echantillon,' she chanted.

'Stop it!' Bev cried nervously.

'She's castin' a spell or somethin'!' Angie said, moving away. 'I don't like this.'

Bev and Angie ran past Lil and darted back through the passageway. But Tracy wasn't so easily intimidated.

'Pathetic!' she yelled after them before glaring at Lil, who was still drawing shapes in the air and muttering strange words.

Tracy swung Verne's rucksack round with all her strength and threw it as far as she could into the white foaming waters. It vanished into the deep. Verne cried out in dismay and Tracy laughed like a donkey.

'Little kids,' she said, striding past Lil. 'You're both saddo losers.' And she jabbed the girl sharply in the side with her elbow.

Lil turned on her, but before she could do anything there was a rumble far out at sea. The storm that had been threatening all afternoon was about to break. The waves smashed with more fury against the pier and one huge swell raced towards them. Tracy screamed as it broke over the stone wall, right where she stood, drenching her from head to toe. Seawater poured from her sleeves and sloshed in the hood of her coat. For several sopping moments she could only gag and spit out the brine that had crashed into her mouth. Then she saw what the great wave had deposited at her feet. It was Verne's rucksack.

Tracy spluttered with disbelief and she stared back at Lil and Verne with bulging eyes. The wave hadn't touched them.

'What *are* you?' she said fearfully as she stumbled away. 'You're not normal! They should bring back burning!'

Lil and Verne watched her stumble and squelch out of sight, back into the town. Then Lil helped the boy to his feet and retrieved his rucksack for him as he loosened his scarf.

'She's such an ignoramus,' she said with irritation. 'They didn't burn witches in England. You all right, Verne? Maybe I should've made you a bobble hat for Christmas instead of that scarf. You can't throttle someone with a woolly hat.'

'How did you do that?' he asked, amazed.

'It's easy. You just cast on and get knitting.'

'No. I mean summon that wave to bring my bag

up from the bottom of the river and soak Tracy?'

Lil laughed. 'Don't be daft!' she said. 'That was just a massive, freaky coincidence.'

'But those words, the spell . . .'

'That wasn't a spell, you thicky. They were knitting terms and types of wool! I wouldn't waste good Latin on that lot. Besides, I keep telling you – there's no such thing as magic. My mum and dad might think they're witches, but that doesn't make it true! Still, it should keep her off your back for a while. She's a nasty piece of work.'

The boy eyed her doubtfully as he hoisted his wet bag on to one shoulder. Wearing that long black velvet cloak, Lil looked entirely capable of commanding the sea to do her bidding.

She glanced at the darkening sky. The low clouds were trawling a curtain of rain towards the harbour.

'We'd best get out of this,' she said, taking his hand. 'Come back to ours and get dry. There's cake.'

High on Whitby's East Cliff, in the old churchyard, the biting wind whipped round the church of St Mary and raged between the hundreds of blackened headstones. The day was getting darker and the sea and the clouds were the same threatening brownish-grey. The storm was gathering in strength. When its full force hit the small seaside town, it would be brutal. The streets below were empty now; everyone had sought shelter.

But through the graveyard a lone, slender figure was creeping. The bright pink raincoat the woman wore almost glowed in the deepening gloom. Stealthily, she threaded her way across the clifftop, staring searchingly at the worn tombstones.

'Gotta be one here someplace,' Cherry Cerise muttered to herself, pushing a pair of large retro sunglasses further up her nose. 'Those little critters love a foul day like this. This is precisely the sort of soaker that always brings them out. So where are . . . ?'

She halted suddenly and caught her breath as a long grey feather blew into her face. Brushing it away, she saw it was streaked with blood. The woman smiled grimly. Gulls were a favourite snack of squalbiters. Another feather rushed by, then another and she stared across the churchyard to where they had come from.

Clinging to the corner of one of the headstones, digging its hind claws into the pitted surface, was a repulsive creature – a squalbiter, just what she was looking for. Cherry had read descriptions of them in the books she kept in a locked drawer back at her cottage, but this was the first time she'd got close to a live one. They were amphibious vermin; vicious imps from the deep regions of the sea, only surfacing to bask in the most violent storms. One of the books contained an old engraving, but even that hadn't prepared her for the ugly reality.

It was the size of a small terrier, and covered in

black and silver scales. Barbed spines ran down a ridged back to the tip of its hooked tail. The four yellow, fishlike eyes in its flat face were fixed on the twitching remains of the bird grasped in its front claws. As Cherry watched, the squalbiter tore off the gull's head and chewed and crunched it noisily, swallowing the tasty mouthful beak first.

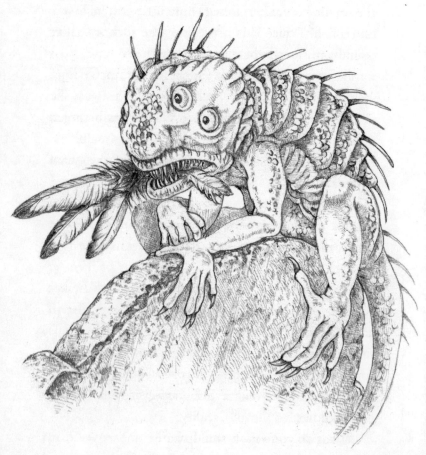

The sea imp was so preoccupied with its meal that Cherry managed to sneak up unnoticed. She lunged forward. Before the creature could react, she caught it in a purple net bag.

Dropping the gull, it let out a scream, reaching through the gaps to attack the human who had captured it. Cherry held the bag at arm's length and the squalbiter's talons raked empty air.

'You play nice,' she warned. 'Else I'll swing this round and smash you against the stone so hard, your nasty carcass will resemble a mess of dropped eggs. You hear me?'

The squalbiter continued to struggle and it began chewing through the purple string.

'Hey!' Cherry protested. 'That's a Mary Quant original!'

Whirling the bag in a wide arc, she crashed it against the headstone, more as a warning than with any real force. Even so, the creature within screamed and pulled its limbs inside, whimpering.

'That's better,' the woman said. 'You be a good little monster or I'll turn you into a gull buffet. If they'd even go near your stinky guts.'

Through the netting, the yellow eyes blazed at her and a snarl gargled behind the rows of sharp teeth.

'Zeer knows you,' a thin, rasping voice hissed. 'Zeer knows.'

'What do you know, squidbreath?'

The creature's thin tongue flicked out at her.

'Witch,' it said.

Cherry's jaw tightened.

'Who told you that?' she demanded.

'Zeer hears much,' came the snickering rely.

'What else did you hear? Tell me about this storm blowin' in. This ain't natural. I know there's somethin' awful behind it, somethin' stronger than I ever sensed before.'

'Yes,' the creature said with a vile grin. 'Very strong. Zeer likes it much.'

'Who sent it and why?'

'Won't tell. You do well to worry.'

'Want me to wallop you again?'

The squalbiter flinched and shook its ugly head.

'Not safe to tell,' it said flatly. 'Crunch my bones, witch. That better than Zeer telling.'

'Well now,' Cherry declared, intensely curious, 'what could possibly be worse than getting your brains bashed in? I'm just gonna have to find out the hard way.'

'Zeer not tell!'

'Keep calm, buster,' she said. 'This won't hurt a bit. I'm just gonna step inside your head and have a look around – I'll even wipe my feet, psychically speaking of course.'

With her free hand, she removed the oversized sunglasses, revealing startlingly pale blue eyes. The squalbiter gibbered and wriggled frantically, trying to hide its face, but it was no use. The urgent movements faltered under the power of Cherry's gaze. Its four round, fishlike eyes were now the palest blue.

'I am Zeer,' Cherry murmured in a remote voice and the thin lips of the squalbiter moved in unison with her words. 'I swim the dark deep. Hate . . . hate fills the waters. Such anger has never been. Hate for this place. For the insult long ago. There are voices in the fathomless trenches. Vengeance. The old grievance. It rankles more than ever. There can be no peace. Secrets. Whitby must pay and the way has been found. The Nimius curse will be roused. Long-dead enemies will awaken. Their quarrel will burn fiercer than before. Melchior Pyke and Scaur Annie will rise again to fight. Two hosts have been chosen. All shall suffer, before the final end . . .'

Cherry let out a strangled gasp and staggered against a headstone as a power greater than she had ever encountered severed the link. The bag dropped from her hand and the squalbiter squirmed free.

'Now you see!' it spat, its yellow eyes glaring at her. 'Now you see!'

'It can't be!' she cried, aghast. 'The promise.' She clutched at the largest of her many bracelets. It was a thick bronze ring, set with three ammonites. 'The Lords of the Deep and Dark,' she whispered fearfully. 'They are forbidden. Whitby is protected.'

Zeer flicked out its tongue, taunting her. 'The

ban has grown weak,' it said. 'The storm that comes carries much power. Their power . . . the Lords of the Deep and Dark have decreed it.'

'But the Nimius has never been found. Even I thought it was just a myth!'

The creature shrieked with mocking laughter. 'This very night the Nimius will emerge from its long hiding and bring about the final end.'

'What . . . what will happen?'

Zeer crawled towards her.

'Cliff shall strive against cliff,' it said. 'Annie and Melchior will do battle and this time everyone shall die. The river will flow thick with blood.'

'And then?'

The squalbiter licked its teeth. 'The cliffs will crumble and fall into the waves. The sea shall devour. Whitby will be no more.'

'There must be a chance,' Cherry said in horror. 'Some way to avert it – to appease Them?'

Zeer tilted its head to gaze up at the glowering sky. The first splashes of rain had started to fall.

'Too late,' it said, grinning horribly. 'The power is upon us. Your time is over. You will be the last witch of Whitby. There will *be* no Whitby.'

The wind grew stronger and Zeer crowed with glee. With a last triumphant glance at Cherry Cerise, the creature darted through the long grass and leaped off the cliff edge. Frilled webs of skin fanned out

12

beneath its long, skinny arms and it rode the fierce gale, sailing over the church tower and out of sight.

Clutching the headstones for support, Cherry stumbled away. She was shaken and mortally afraid. Against the Lords of the Deep and Dark there was nothing she nor anyone else could do. But she had to try. To defend this small seaside town from supernatural attack had been the solemn duty of every Whitby witch for thousands of years.

1

'Is that mouse poo?'

Verne didn't get an answer so he turned from the suspect deposits on the window sill to the kitchen table. Lil was carefully placing a batch of home-made polymer clay badges on a baking tray.

'Ten green witchy faces, with pointy hats,' she declared proudly as she slid them into the oven and clicked the timer round. 'At four quid each in the shop, that's forty quid and I get to keep thirty of it – not bad. If I can make another hundred before the next big Goth Weekend, I'll be minted.'

'Mouse poo?' Verne repeated.

Lil shrugged.

'They always come in from the cliff in bad

15

weather,' she told him. 'We can't leave anything out, like bread or biscuits or even bags of pasta. Mum swears she saw one with pale blue eyes and insists it was a paranormal visitation so she won't use traps, and Sally can't chase them any more, so we're stuck with them.'

Verne wrinkled his nose at the droppings; they didn't look remotely supernatural to him. Crouching down, he stroked the old West Highland terrier in her basket. Sally rolled over to let him tickle her tum.

The boy cast his eyes round the Wilsons' eccentric orange and black kitchen. It was a weird combination of *Macbeth* and IKEA, just what you'd expect from a couple of modern-day witches. He loved coming here. It was the complete opposite of his own home above the amusement arcade where his dust-phobic mother vacuumed the carpets and curtains daily and nothing was ever out of place.

Lil's parents were well known locally, being the owners of an occult shop in Church Street called Whitby Gothic, selling all manner of peculiar and supposedly magical things. They loved dressing the part too, mainly in black with a strong Victorian twist, which they had also foisted on Lil from the day she was born.

Whitby was the perfect place for such a shop. This small seaside town was famous for being the spot where Dracula had landed, bounding off a wrecked ship in the form of a large black dog. But it boasted many other legends and eerie tales of ghosts and monsters. They, combined with the haunting beauty of the ruined abbey and weathered graveyard, high on the East Cliff, attracted seekers of the supernatural and romantic dreamers like a magnet. It was no wonder Lil's parents had grown up to be witches.

'Can't your mum and dad cast a spell to keep the mice away?' Verne asked. 'Or maybe just the non-paranormal ones? That should be peasy magic.'

The girl scowled at him.

'No such thing,' she said for the umpteenth time. 'There's no real witches in Whitby – or anywhere else. Just annoying people like my mum and dad who like to dress up and dance round fires making twits of themselves. Tragic, yes; magic, no.'

Verne wasn't so sceptical, but before he could reply, his stomach growled loudly.

'Borborygmus!' Lil declared.

'What? Is that a magic word, like abracadabra?'

Lil laughed. 'It means belly rumbles,' she explained. 'It's the latest find for my old word collection. I've been dying to use it. Great, isn't it?'

'Where's that cake you promised?'

'Sorry, I was so busy getting my badges ready, I forgot. We've still got plenty left over from my birthday yesterday. My mum might be a bit of a loon, but she's a killer baker.'

Verne agreed. The cake was a moist chocolate sponge, filled with purple butter cream and green jam, topped with a cobweb of yellow icing and twelve black spiders. Mrs Wilson called it *Scrumptious Wickedness*, and it was.

'Make it a big piece,' Verne said as Lil took the lid off a large, rodent-proof tin. 'My mum's on a faddy diet so she can fit into her costume on the Goth Weekend and we've all got to eat the same rabbit food as her so she doesn't get tempted. No pies or chips allowed and absolutely no cake.'

'Your mum doesn't need to diet; she's always jumping about in a tracksuit. And you definitely don't! Why d'you think Tracy Evans calls you "Flimsy"? What's your mum going as – a bonier than usual skeleton?'

'Same as always,' the boy answered, in between mouthfuls. 'Steampunk Edwardian airship pilot in a leather corset with goggles and a ray gun. She was gluing the brass cogs on her flying helmet earlier. And my dad's going as her robot butler. His outfit is almost done. It's going to look look pretty good actually.'

'The way the steampunkers and goths compete with each other over their mad costumes is so funny. The get-ups are more elaborate every time. Nowadays you can't just have a top hat; it has to have smoke coming out of it and flashing lights. And if you're one of the undead, you've got to have movie-quality make-up, preferably with giblets hanging out.'

'Why are our folks so embarrassing?'

Lil grinned. Their eccentric parents had been friends since their schooldays, and now she and Verne were best friends too.

She began tidying away her modelling tools and showed Verne the smart, leather-bound journal she had been given for her birthday. By a happy coincidence, Verne had presented her with a beautiful quill pen, fitted with a biro nib, the feather of which was the same shade of blue as Lil's fringe. Using the pen, Lil had already filled a couple of pages with a list of archaic words discovered in her parents' books. Those forgotten words were fun to say and she was determined to use them in everyday conversation if she got the chance.

'Mirificus,' she read aloud to Verne. 'That means awesomely wonderful, and mulligrubs is when you're feeling down and grumpy.'

'I like mulligrubs!' the boy said, repeating it to himself.

Sally stretched in her basket, then made her way to the back door, glancing backwards to let them know she wanted to go out.

The oven timer pinged. Leaving Verne to remove the badges, Lil pushed the door open for Sally. The wind was so fierce it snatched the handle from her hand and wrenched at the hinges. Lil scrunched her face against the battering rain.

At her feet, the little dog stood still, contemplating the severe weather. Lil gave her an encouraging tap on the bottom and the Westie hopped off the back step and ventured into the wild evening. Lil closed the door hastily and pressed her nose against the glass.

The small garden was hidden by gloom. Beyond the shed, the ground climbed sharply, becoming the sheer slope of the East Cliff. This row of cottages was directly beneath it. Lil couldn't see the top; it was lost in the storm. Up there was the old graveyard that every tourist loved to visit and where the goths regularly draped themselves across crumbling headstones, posing for melodramatic selfies.

'It's horrible out there,' she told Verne. 'I don't think it's going to blow over any time soon.'

'These badges are great,' he said, putting the hot tray on the table. 'Wish I was artistic like you. You draw and make stuff, you knit . . . Stop being so talented, it makes me sick. What'll you do with the money from these?'

'Oh, I've got . . . plans,' Lil said mysteriously. 'Colourful plans.'

Peering through the glass again, she could see no sign of Sally, but it was no use calling for her as the old dog was completely deaf. Lil didn't want to get drenched fetching her in, so she reached for the small torch that hung by the door and shone it towards the far corner of the garden, by the shed. The beam flashed over Sally's milky eyes and the dog came splashing through the puddles. Lil had a towel waiting.

'You're wet and filthy!' the girl scolded.

Sally made contented and playful grunting noises as she let herself be dried. It was one of her favourite games and she was disappointed when Lil stopped.

The noise of the gale outside grew louder, angrier – raging in from the sea and howling down the cliff behind the cottage. The children looked at each other.

'I've never heard anything like that before,' Verne whispered. 'It doesn't sound normal. It's spooky, like screaming ghosts.'

'Don't be soft,' Lil snorted. 'It's just the wind. You'll be saying the weather gods are angry and need placating next – just like my mum.'

'No I won't. I'd say it's the approach of the zombie apocalypse.'

'You're always saying that though.'

'One of these days . . .' the boy said with an exaggerated shiver as he waggled his fingers at her.

The eerie noises outside intensified.

'You want to spend the night on our sofa?' Lil asked. 'You can't get home in this.'

The prospect of staying at the Wilsons all night

appealed, but so did the adventure of battling through the storm. Besides, Verne felt the need to demonstrate some courage after being bullied by Tracy Evans.

'I'll get going now,' he decided. 'Before it gets worse.'

'Wait till Mum and Dad come back from the shop,' Lil suggested, knowing they wouldn't let him slog his way across to the West Cliff alone. 'They'll be here any time. Anyway, all your books are on the radiators.'

But Verne had made up his mind.

'I'll pick them up tomorrow,' he said.

Pulling on his coat and scarf, he slung his still-damp rucksack over his shoulders and hurried through the hall to the front door.

'I really don't think you should go out in that,' Lil cautioned. 'Listen to it!'

'I'll be fine.'

Lil's forehead crinkled with concern, realising she couldn't dissuade him.

'Well, you be careful crossing the bridge!' she said.

'I'm not *that* flimsy! I won't blow away.'

'Text me when you get home safe, yeah?'

Verne waved her worry aside and hurried out into Henrietta Street, but he wasn't prepared for the ferocity of the storm. It was like being hit by an invisible train and he almost went flying. The wind raged up from Tate Hill Sands to tear his breath away and push him violently, pummelling him along. It was frightening and thrilling at the same time. Verne lumbered and staggered and lurched.

The East Cliff was the older half of the town, with many passageways leading off to small courtyards, and the voice of the gale screamed from each opening. As Verne tottered past the foot of the 199 steps that led up to the graveyard and ruined abbey, the tempest came barrelling down them, knocking him sideways. Horizontal rain mixed with sand and sea spray stung his eyes. Suddenly afraid, Verne tried to turn back to the safety of the Wilsons' cottage, but it was impossible and he was driven further up the street.

The narrow ways were deserted. Shop signs swung wildly, while lamp posts shuddered, their quivering lights shaking the shadows. A large awning over a cafe was buckling, pulling on its fixings. A roof tile came crashing down in front of him, car alarms blared and window boxes were snatched from ledges, exploding like mortar shells on the cobbles below.

Suddenly there was a rending of metal as the awning was ripped from the wall. It flew across the street, shattering windows and wrecking shopfronts as it twisted and rolled. Hearing the noise, Verne whipped round, just in time to see the tangle of steel and tattered canvas careering straight for him.

Yelling, he raced away, but the heavy awning came banging and smashing after, riding the wind faster than he could run. Spinning and rebounding from one side of the street to the other, it bore down on him. The flailing steel struts whirled round like the runaway blades of a combine harvester, gouging chunks from walls and striking sparks from the ground. Verne knew he'd be killed if he didn't get out of its way.

With a desperate spurt of energy, he leaped aside into the turning for Market Place and dodged behind one of the broad pillars there. The awning rampaged by, chiselling deep cuts in the stone exactly where his head had been. It thundered along, until its lethal progress was halted when it smashed into the windscreen of a parked van.

Catching his breath, Verne stumbled on. Hurrying down the even narrower passage of Sandgate, he approached what he knew would be the most dangerous part of this nightmare journey. Steeling himself, he rounded the corner and faced the swing bridge that spanned the River Esk.

In that exposed spot, the gale was stronger than ever. It came sweeping in off the sea, throwing the boats in the harbour about like bath toys. The sheltering piers were no protection. Waves came crashing between them; whipped white and deadly by the squall, they charged up the seething river. Bales of foam surged over the harbour wall and streaked across the road, scattering in the storm. With bitter irony, Verne recalled what he had said to Lil. The possibility of being swept away was a very real one. He stared fearfully at the bridge ahead, where the waves were lashing through the railings, and let out a cry of surprise.

There was a woman on the bridge.

Even through the driving rain and the blizzard of foam flecks, Verne recognised her. No one else in Whitby dressed like that. It was Cherry Cerise, whom all the children laughed at. She was wearing a shocking-pink plastic raincoat, with a matching hood tied tightly under her chin and the nylon tresses of an orange wig were streaming wildly behind.

She was standing in the exact centre of the bridge, facing the harbour mouth while wrathful waves broke around her. Miss Cerise was in her sixties and more than a bit strange, but Verne had never seen her do anything as weird as this before. He wondered if she was all right. She was perfectly still. Perhaps she was paralysed with fear.

Forgetting his own terrors, he ventured on to the bridge, wading through the seething sea foam and clutching hold of the grilled railing. The bridge was juddering alarmingly.

'Hello!' he bawled, trying to make himself heard above the tempest. 'Hello! Are you OK? Do you need help? You have to get off the bridge. Go home!'

It was only when he drew close to her that she noticed him. The woman turned her pale face, eyes covered by rhinestone-rimmed sunglasses.

'Who are you?' she cried. 'Scram, kid!'

'You can't stay here!' he yelled back. 'Where do you live? Let me help you.'

Cherry Cerise jerked her head around and raised her hands as if to ward off the storm.

'You hear that?' she shouted manically. 'There's voices on the air. Powers are wakin', kid – dark powers! Resentment! Hate! Vengeance!'

Verne couldn't hear anything but the clamour of the storm.

'Come away!' he pleaded, but the woman grabbed his shoulders and shook him roughly.

'Run, kid!' she shrieked in his face. 'Save your own skin! But you won't escape. None of us can! The ruin of everything has started!'

Verne pulled himself free and it was then he saw that she had tied herself to the railing with the belt of her raincoat.

A huge wave came smashing over the bridge, drenching them both. For the second time that day, Verne was thrown to the ground.

Cherry Cerise leaned into the gale and started singing.

'You're off your head!' the boy yelled at her.

He didn't wait any longer. If she wanted to get soaked and risk her life out here, that was her business. At least he'd tried to help.

Clinging to the other railing, he made his way across the bridge and ran on to the quayside of the West Cliff. He was almost home. Before rushing there, he paused and turned back for one final glimpse of the deranged woman.

Verne blinked and rubbed his eyes. Strange lights seemed to be shining from her hands. Bright colours were pulsing and glowing over her outstretched palms. The boy shook his head and backed away. It was an insane night; he must be seeing things. He was exhausted and anxious to get indoors – and he couldn't wait to text Lil.

At the Wilsons, Lil had carried Sally upstairs because the steps were too steep for her. As usual, the little dog had broken wind all the way, a habit that had earned her the nickname 'furry bagpipe'.

Changing out of her school uniform, Lil viewed the contents of her wardrobe with a scowl.

'I have got to get rid of these drab clothes and cloaks,' she said. 'I'm sick of the whole goth thing. I've been shoved into bodices and black lace since I was a baby. I need some bright colours in my life.'

She cast her eyes round her bedroom. The walls were a dark blood-red and the woodwork and ceiling were black. It was high time for a change – and not just for her. She was close to launching a daring scheme, which the money from the badges would help fund. By the time she was done, Whitby would be a blaze of colour and the forthcoming Goth Weekend would have the gloominess slapped out of it.

Delving into the back of her wardrobe, she reached for a large bag filled with balls of wool and colourful knitting. Lil was a fast and skilled knitter. She made witchy tea cosies and other woolly novelties for the shop, but this stash was part of her secret plan. She wasn't the only one who was fed up with the austere black costumes that thronged the streets. Lil was sure the locals would appreciate her campaign to brighten up their hometown.

Before she could pull the bag out, her mobile rang. Lil hoped it was Verne, but it was her mother.

'You all right there, luv?' Mrs Wilson asked. 'Your dad and me are stuck in the shop waiting for this shocking weather to ease off.'

'Yeah, I'm fine,' the girl answered.

'If you're scared on your own I can send your father over. I've drawn a chalk circle round him, performed a protection spell, given him my rain hood and put a sachet of rowan under it so he doesn't get struck by lightning, and he's chewing some ginger that he can spit into the wind and ward off the worst of it, so he'll be OK.'

'He'll get soaked! Don't send him out in this. I'm not frightened of a stupid storm. Besides, I'm not on my own; I've got Sal here.'

'Fat lot of good she is. Now are you sure, darling? Because I've been casting the runes as well and they say something terrible is going to happen.'

'Oh, Mother, stop it.'

'This is no ordinary storm, Lil. It's a warning – or worse.'

'Save that for the customers.'

'Light a votive candle and invoke the forces of protection like I've showed you.'

'Bye, Mum. Gotta go.'

Lil ended the call. Her mum was always a bit over the top and right now Lil could do without the melodrama. She checked her phone for texts, but there were none. She hoped Verne was OK. He should have reached home by now.

The storm outside was louder than ever. Her bedroom window rattled furiously in the frame and, in spite of her scepticism, the girl felt a cold shiver run down her spine. Maybe her mother was right. There was something strange and unnatural about the ferocity of this weather. The hairs rose on the back of her neck and Lil began to feel afraid.

Although she was deaf and half blind, Sally had also sensed something was wrong. The little Westie was gazing up at the window, head tilted and ears flicking. A low growl started in her throat. That in itself was unnerving: Sally was a very quiet dog and hardly ever barked.

'It's all right,' Lil said, trying to reassure the pair of them. 'It'll blow itself out soon.'

Sally rose slowly. Her tail was down and she

31

became rigid, her lips pulling into a snarl.

'Don't worry, Sal. We'll be fine. It's just the silly old wind; nothing to –'

As she spoke, there was a loud splintering and Sally started to bark.

Lil ran to the window. Looking down, she saw the roof of the shed being ripped from its sides and go spinning across neighbouring gardens. Sally barked even louder and darted forward. Clamping her teeth on the leg of Lil's jeans, she pulled as hard as she could.

Lil barely noticed. Plant pots were shooting from the unroofed shed like rockets and one of the walls had lifted off the base. It flipped over the garden wall and sailed sideways.

'Unreal,' she breathed.

Sally let go of the denim. She barked some more, but when that had no effect, she pushed her nose under the trouser leg and nipped the girl's ankle.

Lil yelped as the dog reclamped her jaws to her jeans and started to drag her away from the window, forcing the girl to hop after.

There was an almighty rumble, louder and deeper than any sound Lil had ever heard. It juddered right through her and the pain in her ankle was forgotten. The house shook as a massive slice of the cliff face calved away and came thundering down the slope, on to the Wilsons' garden. Soil and stones slammed against the cottage and Lil's bedroom window exploded inwards. The spot where she had been standing only moments before was speared with broken glass and rubble. The gale came screeching into the room, whipping up the bedding, wrenching the curtains from the rail and scattering yesterday's birthday cards.

Sally resumed her urgent, frightened barking as she backed against the door, with Lil frozen and gawping by her side. As she stared, a text beeped into Lil's phone.

Finally back!!! OMG u won't believe what just happened!!!!

In the midst of her fear, Lil almost laughed. She looked around at the devastation and prepared to take a photo of it to send to Verne. Then she saw the scene outside the gaping window and her mouth fell open.

The darkness was choked with swirling debris, and other things that had been seized by the unnatural hurricane. Ancient coffins had been ripped from the exposed ground high above. They bounced down the collapsed cliff, rupturing and splitting open, spilling their occupants and surrendering them to the ferocious wind. Now dozens of nightmarish figures were flying in the sky. Old bones, some still wrapped in the tattered remnants of the clothes they had been buried in, were whirling through the air like autumn leaves. Skeletons somersaulted and tumbled on the wind, colliding, entangling, spinning round each other as though

performing some ghastly, supernatural dance. Sticklike arms flailed, legs kicked and skulls were thrown back as jaws sprang open. They appeared gruesomely alive.

Lil raised her phone and started filming that eerie waltz. This was better than Verne's zombie apocalypse. But it was too dark for the figures to show up on the screen. Lil scowled and moved a little closer to the shattered window. She changed the camera settings and the shapes began to emerge. Zooming in, it showed billowing, ragged shrouds and rotted scraps of Sunday suits streaming like ribbons. The unearthly gale made marionettes of the skeletons. They pirouetted in a maniacal ballet, swooping low over the garden, then plucked up once more to spin above the roofs.

'Now *that* is mirificus,' the girl murmured.

The funnelling wind tore round and round and the collisions became more violent. The bodies began to disintegrate as the brittle, mummified flesh and sinew that bound them snapped in the storm. Arms fell out of sleeves and heads spun away from necks.

Anxious not to miss a moment, Lil continued to record. The one body that remained intact seemed to be looking straight at the lens. There was something foul and wicked about that dead face with its long, lank hair and Lil didn't like it. There was malice in the blank eye sockets and the jaw was waggling as if with laughter. Lil tried to keep from shivering with revulsion to maintain a steady picture. Verne would never believe it. She didn't believe it herself.

The phone began to zoom in on that hideous skull and Lil frowned in irritation and tried to correct it. Too late the girl realised it wasn't the phone at all – the skeleton was racing towards her.

The fearful corpse came crashing through the broken window, bony hands reaching out. Lil didn't have time to scream. That terrible face smacked into hers. The skull struck her forehead so violently she was thrown to the floor. A blast of decay blew from the open mouth into her own and the mane of dirty hair wrapped about her head. The phone slid from Lil's fingers and she lay unconscious, insensible to the storm and Sally's frantic barking – and yet she was aware of a creeping, unnatural cold that entered her mind, and with it a hissing voice.

'Know me,' it said. 'In life, I was Scaur Annie. See that what my eyes saw; make my ears yours. Drink full my spite and hate. We two shall be one. Melchior Pyke's power is waking. We must stop him. He shall not win, not this time. Scaur Annie will thwart him again.'

'Scaur Annie . . .' Lil murmured.

'Live them days long buried, long dead,' the voice inside her head commanded. 'You be Scaur Annie. See what I saw. Hear what I heard.'

'I . . .' Lil breathed. 'We . . . us . . . be Scaur Annie.'

Outside, the squalling gale began to die down. Lil's head lolled to one side and she remained motionless as her mind went journeying back, to relive the events of a summer night that was filled with anger and fear four hundred years ago.

She opened her eyes to savage, angry yells, and scrambled backwards on all fours. But she wasn't Lil any more and she wasn't in her bedroom. Hundreds of years had peeled away. She was Scaur Annie, a seventeen-year-old barefoot girl in a coarse woollen kirtle and a tattered smock.

A guttering rushlight illuminated the interior of a humble wooden shack, built on the grassy slope of the cliff, with ragged hangings to keep out the biting gales. Bunches of drying herbs and seaweed were suspended from the sloping roof; beautiful shells and the skeleton of a two-headed lamb dangled among them. Clay pots and jars were ranged against one of the walls, and a rough straw mattress covered in sacking lay by another. It was dark outside, but harsh voices filled the night.

'Come out, you filthy-faced hag!'

'Best you do, or we must come in and fetch.'

'Shall we drag you out by your hair an' beat you with sticks?'

'Step out and make answer!'

'Witch!'

Scaur Annie scrambled into a corner of the hut, pulling her knees under her chin.

'Get gone from my door!' she cried. 'Get gone, masters – else I'll have at you. I'll pray long an' loud at Them what rule under the waves. Them'll send shadows to pull you under. Your boats'll be upended and you'll drown in the cruel salt deep. Nowt but widows and bairns'll be left. Think on it!'

The hostile shouts and threats outside turned to anxious murmurs.

'She's workin' up to ill-wish an' grief-charm us,' one of them said fearfully.

'We must stop her 'fore she spells it!'

'Aye. Burn the witch in her den. Fire will staunch her evil. Lob your lanterns at it.'

Annie heard a lantern crash against her door. The oil splashed across the timbers and at once greedy flames leaped between them. Another lantern struck the roof and rolled all the way across, dropping down behind the back wall, leaving a burning trail in its wake.

The girl shrieked and clutched at the talisman of three ammonites around her neck.

'Save us!' she implored. 'O Ye mighty powers of the deep, Ye Three Lords under foam and wave – save this Your servant, Scaur Annie. Deliver her from fires. Send a knight to shield and guard her. Hear me, an' ever more I'll do Your bidding, by sky, sand and sea – I swears it.'

The flames were roaring around her now. Choking black smoke stung her eyes and her long, matted hair was smouldering in the intense heat. The shack began to buckle and collapse. One of the blazing roof planks came crackling down inside. Annie screeched and her tattered skirts caught fire.

In that terrifying, scorching moment, she heard a stern, commanding voice yell out and the burning door was ripped away. A tall, cloaked figure braved the leaping flames and strode into the inferno. She felt strong hands rip the fiery rags from her body, then carry her outside.

Cold night air filled her gasping lungs and her eyes were blurred and streaming. The rescuer carried her down the steep slope to the beach and laid her gently on the sand. Then he removed his cloak and covered her nakedness.

Peering up, Annie tried to look on him, but her vision was watery. All she could make out was an imposing figure in a high black hat. Behind him, on the grassy ridge, her hovel blazed fiercely and nearby was a crowd of scared and angry men, bearing sticks and boathooks.

'Peace be on you, mistress,' her saviour said. 'None

shall harm you now. You have my solemn pledge.'

'She's a witch!' the mob cried. 'Cast her back into the flames. Let her evil be scourged from our land.'

Drawing his sword, the stranger rounded on them.

'Whosoever lays hands on this girl will feel the bite of my steel,' he promised. 'What is this madness?'

The men eyed the weapon doubtfully. They were simple fishermen and farmers, unused to facing gentlemen with swords. The flames shone brightly over the blade and the sight cut through their righteous fury. Lowering their eyes, they grew silent and shuffled their feet – except for one.

'Who are you to flout the Almighty's justice?' a sharp voice demanded.

The crowd parted and the unmistakable figure of a Puritan strode forward. His face was grim and sour and he was uncowed by the blade that swung round to point at him.

'I am Sir Melchior Pyke, natural philosopher, scholar and, at this moment, a whisker's breadth away from adding butcher to my accomplishments,' Annie's protector thundered, and the authority in his voice caused many to gasp and stare. 'What justice is here? I see none. Here is but a wretched girl cruelly wronged.'

'Wronged?' the Puritan cried. 'Did you not hear? That foul hussy is in the devil's service. Her mother was a witch and so is she. She is an abhorrence in the eyes of the Lord.'

'I heard naught but frightened sheep bleating foolish accusations, and now I perceive that you are the shepherd who drives them to commit murder.'

'Shepherd?' the Puritan repeated with pride. 'Aye, I am John Ashe, licensed preacher, and this is my flock.'

'Whitby folk?'

'Nay, Master,' Annie spoke up from the folds of the cloak. 'Them's from Sandsend and yonder. There's none in Whitby would hurt their Annie.'

'Stay silent, witch!' the preacher commanded, flinging sand at her face.

'Do that again and I shall fillet you,' her saviour growled.

'You spoke of sheep,' the Puritan said, undaunted. 'Amen to that. Tom Brooksby, stand forth.'

A stout, bald-headed man edged forward, not daring to meet the stern gaze of the man with the sword. Muttering under his breath, he explained he farmed a modest plot near Goathland. With a quick glance at Annie, he related how, yesterday, he caught her trespassing and chased her away. That night he was tormented by evil dreams in which she danced with a black ram and that morning he found two of his sheep dead.

''Twas her doing an' no mistake,' he said bitterly.

'And them's not the first to be killed in the dead of night!' called another. 'There's many who've lost livestock.'

'A wild dog is the most likely cause,' Melchior Pyke stated. 'As for your dreams, Tom Brooksby, they are the busy night's work of your own conscience and ale-soaked fancies.'

'All know she's a witch and more!' the preacher declared hotly.

'And I say unto you, where are your proofs of malice? It'll be the assizes for all if you dare harm this girl – and thence the drop.'

'Proofs?' the preacher cried. 'There are ways of obtaining such proofs. Stand aside and I shall provide them. I have learning in these matters.'

The sword jerked to the man's throat and nicked a ribbon of blood from his neck. The preacher recoiled and the crowd murmured unhappily.

'The law of King James allows it,' the Puritan spluttered indignantly. 'His own work, his *Daemonologie*, is most clear . . .'

'Do not throw His Majesty's name at me! I am lately come from Scottish Jimmy's court. I know the king well and account him friend and patron. Before you cite any more of the king's works, know that I assisted with the translation of his own Bible!'

The claim drew astonished cries from everyone and any lingering resistance was quashed.

'Friend of the king,' they whispered in awe. 'An' a right holy one at that.'

John Ashe studied the man's face as if for the first

time. He was surely not yet thirty years of age, his handsome features were strong with character and an intelligence as keen as his sword blade glinted in his steel-grey eyes.

'I must yield to your greater learning,' the Puritan said humbly. 'Pray forgive any imprudence on my part.'

'I do not call an attempted burning "imprudence",' the man replied sternly. 'Yet you beg pardon of the wrong person. It was not I whom you wronged.'

The Puritan looked down at the cloaked girl with displeasure.

'The Almighty has watched over you this night,' he said coldly. 'Give thanks for His boundless mercy. Take learning from it and leave the paths of wickedness.'

Annie glowered up at him and spat.

'That was no apology,' her rescuer agreed. 'Now get gone from this place; you have done enough evil work this night. But hear me, all of you: restitution must be made. You will catch no fish, nor tend your beasts, till you have built a new home and furnished it to this lady's liking. You will begin at first light, so bring timber and tools. Am I understood?'

The crowd grumbled and John Ashe shook his head in defiance.

'And you, preacher,' Melchior Pyke instructed, 'will bear the expense of those things that are not so easily replaced or remade, from your own purse.'

'You overreach yourself!' he objected.

Many in the crowd agreed with him and their initial fear of the stranger was beginning to fade.

'He can't make us do that,' some of them mumbled.

'Oh, I can,' he assured them. 'If you are not here tomorrow, I will send my manservant to fetch each and every one of you. For your own sakes, I pray you, do not compel me to send him on that errand. He is not so patient as I – are you, Mister Dark?'

He had called out, past the crowd, and they turned to see whom he was addressing.

A tall, wiry-looking man in a long black coat had crept up silently behind them and they drew in their breath when he stepped into the firelight.

No one had ever seen flesh so grey and cadaverous on a living man. His eyes were set deep under heavy brows, across which thick black hair bristled in a single unbroken line. His nose was long but crushed to one side and his mouth was wide and downturned, with thin, cruel lips. Grains of gunpowder were embedded in his cheeks like seeds, and a rough, jagged scar ran down the right side of his face, through his lips and down to his chin. Bound about his throat, tucked under his collar, was a thin scarf of grubby green silk, but it couldn't disguise his misshapen neck. A nub of bone protruded from under the skin, where the marks of an old rope burn were still clearly visible.

At the sight of him, half the mob hurried away and

the rest followed when he pulled a snaplock pistol from his belt.

John Ashe was visibly shaken and he turned back to Melchior Pyke.

'Now I know you, my lord,' he declared. 'There has been talk of this crook-necked man. He has gained an ungentle reputation in the alehouses, and what is it you do, locked away in your rooms behind The White Horse?'

'Science,' Melchior Pyke answered flatly.

'Science, is it?' the Puritan snorted. 'What science could guide you to Whitby?'

'I was invited here to discover a more efficient method of extracting alum from the local shale.'

'Is that why those foul, sulphurous reeks hang over The White Horse?'

'Verily, sulphuric acid is essential to the process. Or are you ignorant enough to believe I was summoning Old Nick in those outbuildings?'

The Puritan blustered and pointed an accusatory finger at Mister Dark.

'What manner of science drives your trained walking corpse to tramp the shore at night?' he demanded. 'He has been sighted; do not deny it.'

At that moment, there was a flash and a small explosion as Mister Dark fired the pistol close to the Puritan's head.

John Ashe sprang back and glared at them both.

'King's friend ye may be,' he said, 'but King James is a long way from here. Tread with caution, my lord. I have you under my observance now. John Ashe shall know what truly brings you hither, with such a misbegotten creature as this – and why you give protection to witches. Aye, these things I shall discover.'

He turned his back in a deliberate snub and strode off towards Sandsend, following the fleeing crowd.

'There's the fuse of trouble set smouldering,' Melchior Pyke observed. ''Tis a blessed fortune my work here is almost done.'

Looking down at the girl he had rescued, he helped her to stand.

'All that were mine in this world were in there,' she uttered, staring at the dying flames. 'Weren't much, but it were mine.'

'Then until those villains make reparation, we must disregard the proprieties and invite you to our lodgings, mistress,' he said cheerfully. 'I know there is a supper waiting, to which you are most welcome, and we shall hunt you out fresh clothing. Come, take my arm.'

Scaur Annie wasn't used to kindness from lordly folk. She gazed into his handsome face and tried to read his purpose.

'I saved your life,' he reminded her gently. 'I have travelled through many countries; in some of them, that very act decrees you are now my property.'

The girl pulled away. 'I can flit fast as a rabbit,' she boasted defiantly. 'You'll never catch me. I know places where no one would never find me.'

Melchior Pyke laughed. 'Calm yourself. I seek only to feed and clothe you – naught else. There is no reason to be afraid.'

So Annie allowed herself to be coaxed and she walked beside him, along the sands, towards Whitby.

Behind them, the sinister Mister Dark cast his eyes up and down the shore and over the grassy cliff. He thought he caught sight of a small, weather-beaten face watching from behind a rock, but it was gone in an instant.

A low, threatening growl sounded in his throat as he recognised it as one of those strange creatures who lived in the caves beneath the cliff. Melchior Pyke's main intent in coming to Whitby was to speak with those legendary aufwaders, who alone possessed the knowledge vital to his true work. However, those small, secretive beings had so far evaded Mister Dark and his irritation had turned to anger.

His eyes glinted as he stared into the night. Now perhaps there was a chance. Scaur Annie had the complete trust of those creatures; he had witnessed the young witch speaking to them several times. His master's new plan was to use her to approach them.

Mister Dark grinned unpleasantly. Sir Melchior

Pyke had inveigled his way into the most strongly guarded libraries of distant empires and enticed the deepest mysteries from the wise; he would certainly be able to charm a low, beggarly girl into doing his bidding.

As he turned to leave, Mister Dark rasped his thumb and forefinger together, and crackling whiskers of blue fire spat from his hand.

3

Verne sat back in the little change booth, surrounded by the raucous din and flashing lights of his family's amusement arcade. It was so mean of his father to make him do this Saturday morning shift when everything was happening across the river on the East Cliff.

'What happened then?' he asked urgently, speaking into the phone clamped to his ear.

Lil's voice rattled on, hardly stopping for breath.

'So I come to, with Sally barking like mad and this stinking skeleton right on top of me!'

'No! What did you do?'

'I booted it off and the head went rolling under my bed. I grabbed Sally and we legged it out of there.'

'That is so awesome. And you say the telly wants to interview you? When's that happening?'

'They'll be here any minute. Come over. It looks like a bomb went off!'

Verne rested his head on the counter in front of him and groaned. 'I can't budge till twelve,' he said. 'My folks aren't back yet. It's just me here.'

'All your lot are over here, having a gawp.'

'What? That is so not fair!'

'So many gongoozlers, you wouldn't believe it.'

'So many what?'

'Gongoozlers.'

'That one of your funny old words?'

'Yes, it means an idle spectator. The street's packed with them right now.'

'I'd like to do some gongoozling myself.'

'Can't you close up and pop over for ten minutes? The skellies are going to be taken away soon. They're all in bits across the back gardens.'

'Nooo! Don't let them till I've had a look!'

'Get a move on then!'

Lil ended the call and Verne gave a forlorn whimper.

'I've got the mulligrubs,' he uttered.

He replayed the footage Lil had sent him and felt a pang of envy that even the frightening final seconds of the lunging cadaver couldn't scare away. Glancing over at a sulky-looking woman on the push-and-drop amusement, he wished the teetering coins would cascade into her handbag so she'd leave. They didn't and she was soon in front of his booth for the fourth time that morning, demanding change for a fiver.

As Verne was passing across yet more piles of ten-pence pieces, they were both startled by the noisy jingle of falling coins and she stared back at the machine in gasping outrage. A teenager had usurped her place and a deluge of silver was cascading into the metal gutter in front of him.

'That's mine!' she snapped, marching up to the boy, tight-lipped with fury. 'You're stealing my money!'

The boy looked round in confusion.

'What's up with you?'

'I was on that!' she told him.

'Not when I got here.'

'That money is morally mine!'

'Don't be daft!' he laughed.

'Disgraceful!' she fumed. But unless she actually fought him for the coins, there was nothing more to be done, and he looked more than capable of fighting back. Giving him one final withering glower, she stomped off.

The boy winked at her, which only infuriated her more, and she left the arcade almost frothing at the mouth.

'I hate sore losers,' the boy said, bringing his swag to the booth to convert into notes.

'Thanks a bunch, Clarke,' Verne said, not returning his older brother's cheeky grin. 'That's Tracy Evans's mum. First the boyfriend, now the mother. I'll cop it on Monday. She fed her housekeeping into that machine. That's their Sunday dinner you've got there.'

'Tasty!' the boy laughed.

'You know Dad doesn't like you claim-jumping, Clarke,' Verne said. 'It looks iffy.'

'Oi, I won that fair and square. I didn't know the old misery was playing it. I just saw a load of dosh going begging. Would've been barmy to walk past.'

'He still won't be happy.'

'Well, he's not going to find out, is he?'

Verne gave a crafty smile. 'That depends,' he said. 'If you take my place here for the next hour, I'll forget all about it.'

Clarke laughed. 'No need for blackmail. That's why I came back from the East Cliff. I knew you'd be itching to go have a nose over at Lil's. Don't say I never do nothing for you.'

'Cheers!' Verne said gratefully as he scrambled out of the booth.

'No longer than an hour though!' Clarke called after him. 'I'm taking Amy to Scarborough on the Vespa at half one!'

Verne was already out of the arcade, pulling on his coat and running along Pier Road towards the bridge, wriggling his arms into the straps of his rucksack.

It was the first fine dry day in weeks and the gulls were making the most of it, filling the sky with shrieks and screams. Below them, the sea was calm and the river was quiet. All the fishing boats had put out and the harbour was the emptiest it had been all winter. There was some damage to windows and cars on this side from last night's storm, but Verne wasn't interested in any of that.

Hurrying along the quayside, he looked across to the opposite bank, beyond the red-brick walls and terracotta roofs, up to the long reach of the cliff. Emergency fencing was being installed at the edge of the churchyard. The damaged area where the ground had slipped away was clearly visible. It looked like a huge, ugly bite had been taken out of that grassy ridge. Verne could see tantalising holes in the dark soil, which were almost certainly yawning graves, and figures in hi-vis clothing were conducting a careful search.

'They're collecting the bones already!' he muttered, anxious there'd be nothing to see by the time he got there.

Reaching the small swing bridge, he pushed through the people, busy about their Saturday, and realised he'd forgotten all about his encounter with Cherry Cerise. He wondered how long she had remained bound to the rail last night and what on earth she had been doing.

Running, he made his way into the narrow cobbled lanes of the East Cliff, past the small openings leading to little courtyards, and headed towards Henrietta Street. A determined clean-up operation was taking place, yard brushes were out in force and broken windows had already been boarded over. The van that the awning had smashed into had been towed away and a great crowd had gathered at the bottom of the 199 steps. Verne couldn't get past and he stared upwards to see what was going on.

On one of the flat stages, which had been built into those old steps to let bygone coffin-bearers have a rest on their climb to the churchyard, stood Lil and her mother, Cassandra. They were being interviewed by a TV news crew, with the landslip and the obliterated gardens plain to see behind.

'A sunny day this morning.' Cheeky chappy local news reporter Nigel Hampton addressed the camera. 'A far cry from the scene last night when severe storms battered the north-east coast. But here, in the Yorkshire town of Whitby, famed for its links with Dracula, hurricane-force winds were recorded – and something else too, but more of that in a moment. As you can see behind me, a large section of the waterlogged cliff fell away, causing damage and destruction and forcing many people out of their homes to spend the night in emergency accommodation. Some of the town's oldest inhabitants were also disturbed, as we'll discover. Twelve-year-old Lilith Wilson here saw it all from her bedroom.'

'Lil,' the girl interrupted.

The man smiled. 'Lil, I do apologise. And what a cute little pup you've got.'

The man reached out to pet Sally, who was in Lil's arms. The dog responded by biting his fingers.

'She's not a puppy,' Lil corrected. 'She's almost sixteen and she's deaf and half blind. She doesn't like it when strange hands suddenly loom up at her like that.'

Cassandra Wilson leaned over. 'Startles her you see,' she said. 'You should never try to stroke an unfamiliar dog anyway. You wouldn't like being prodded and pawed at by total strangers, would you? Or maybe you would.'

The reporter's trademark cheeky smile tightened on his face as an audible *parp* tooted from Sally's rear end.

'She gulps her water down,' Lil explained.

'Bless her,' he managed to say. 'So here I am with Lil and Cassandra Wilson in the aftermath of the storm. But before we come on to that, our viewers might be wondering why you're in fancy dress? I thought the big Goth Weekend wasn't for another few weeks.'

Lil's mother gave a dramatic toss of the head. She had spent longer than usual in front of a mirror that morning. Her plump face was powdered pale, with broad, coal-black lines accentuating her eyes and stark blackcurrant lipstick outlining her mouth. A necklace of Whitby jet sat on top of her bosom that had been pushed high under her chin by a black bodice, and a hooded cloak was fastened at her throat by a silver brooch in the shape of a bat.

'It isn't fancy dress,' she announced, with flash of her Cleopatra eyes, and a flourish of her many-ringed fingers. 'I am a witch, as is my husband, and these are just my everyday clothes. What is more, we firmly believe that last night was no ordinary storm. It was supernatural in origin, a sign of some momentous power at work.'

'Witches?' the reporter cut in with a wink to camera. 'With broomsticks and frogs?'

'Are you mocking my faith, Mr Hampton? Please

don't do that. I'm sure you don't want me to file a complaint against you and your station for religious intolerance.'

'No, no!' the man spluttered hastily. 'Please, I meant no offence. But witches, surely . . .?'

'There are plenty of us about,' she told him. 'My shop couldn't survive if it had to rely solely on Goth Weekends. Even in this small town there are three covens and you'd be amazed at how many witches come here for their holidays to soak up Whitby's special atmosphere.'

'Your shop?'

'Whitby Gothic,' Mrs Wilson said, plugging the business shamelessly to the camera. 'It's on Church Street. Caters for all your occult needs, whether that be a scrying crystal, obscure reference books, incense, ritual candles, robes – and yes, even broomsticks and frogs. Check out the shop's website; everything is available online and there's a ten per cent discount if you order today.'

She pointed to the badges she and Lil were both wearing.

'Genuine Whitby witches,' she declared proudly. 'My daughter makes them herself and we sell them. Aren't they wonderful?'

'If we could just get back to what happened last night . . .'

Mrs Wilson grew serious once more. 'Yes,' she

said darkly. 'Ancient forces have undoubtedly been unleashed.'

'Where were you when the cliff collapsed?'

'Me and Mike, my husband, were inside the shop, down the far end of the street, but it was so loud we still heard it. I sensed at once it was something *other*. I had consulted the runes you see. Poor Lil, look at the bruise on her forehead.'

Nigel Hampton turned to Lil. 'Can you describe what you saw?' he asked.

'There was a huge rumble and a massive chunk of the cliff came crashing into our garden,' she told him.

'Obliterated under a mountain of soil,' her mother put in. 'I had all my spring bulbs coming up, and the herbs I use in my potions and philtres – now they're buried under half the cliff.'

'Bit of an exaggeration, Mum,' Lil said.

'We can't return to the cottage until the surveyors say it's safe,' Mrs Wilson continued. 'We had to sleep in the shop last night.'

The reporter turned back to the camera and in his most serious voice said, 'And then something even more bizarre took place. The landslip left many old graves exposed and what can only be described as a tornado came twisting across the gardens below. This is what happened.'

He paused to allow the footage from Lil's phone to be edited into the piece later, then turned to her as if he had only just watched it, instead of three hours earlier when Mrs Wilson had emailed it to the station.

'Chilling to the marrow,' he declared. 'I can't imagine what was going through your head as you recorded that – especially when that skeleton came straight for you. Did you think it was one of the undead? A flying demon? Or black magic?'

'We don't have black magic here!' Mrs Wilson interrupted, bristling indignantly.

'I knew it was only being blown by the wind,' Lil answered, stony-faced. 'But it was still freaky.'

'You weren't scared even a tiny bit?

'Nah!' she fibbed. 'It was just nature going off on one. And this means I get my room redecorated – result!'

'And that nasty bruise is where the skull struck you?'

'Yeah, it really clonked me one and sent me flying, but I gave it a bigger wallop back and knocked its block off.'

'Ancient forces,' Mrs Wilson repeated starkly. 'Old powers are awakening. This is just the start, and I say unto Whitby, beware! I've cast the witch's runes . . . have I already said that?'

'Yes you have.'

'We sell a starter bag for just £12.99.'

The reporter turned to the camera again. 'This is

Nigel Hampton in the spookier than usual town of Whitby.'

He waited a moment, smiling down the lens – a smile that vanished as Mrs Wilson's voice called out, 'You can see that footage again on our shop's website – and don't forget it's discount day.'

'Let's go and talk to the vicar now,' he told the camera guy. 'And we'll need some juicy close-ups of the graves. Skeletons would be heaven, but if they've already been zipped up, let's at least see them being carted off.'

Without bothering to thank the Wilsons for their contribution, Nigel started ascending the steps to the church, grumbling about his knees.

The crowd below began to disperse slowly. Some went about their shopping, but most went to view the damage down Henrietta Street.

'We should get a lot of lovely online trade today,' Mrs Wilson said, rubbing her hands together. 'You'll be famous, Lil. I wonder how many hits that video will get?'

'Can we go home now?' the girl asked. 'I want to have a bath and get changed.'

'Your dad's with the surveyors now. The glazier's mending the window, but your room will need a thorough clean. Will you be OK?'

'How'd you mean "OK"?'

'OK as in there's been a dead body in your bedroom all night long. I'll need to do a purification ritual to cleanse it of negative forces and then place pouches of agrimony on the window sill. It's a herb of virtue and will give protection.'

'A mop and a bucket of hot soapy water would work better. Besides, it doesn't bother me. I've seen worse frights on the Goth Weekends. I'm just looking forward to a proper room makeover.'

'The insurance will cover that,' her mother said. 'You know, Lil, I was thinking – you could really go for it. Sable-black walls, with lush purple curtains, tied back with black ropes with enormous tassels and a lampshade like a bloodshot eye.'

'No, none of that,' Lil said sternly. 'I've had enough haunted-house decor to last a lifetime. I want a total change. I want daffodil walls, a pale blue ceiling and a lime-green door.'

Mrs Wilson pulled a face. 'You're not serious?' she gasped. 'That'd be hideous, like living in a jar of jelly beans.'

'And a white fluffy rug to put my bare feet on,' Lil

said, her voice trailing to a dreamlike murmur. 'Soft and warm when I wake, as the last star leaves the night and the brim of the sea fills with pale fires and the gulls greet the dawn. No more cold sand 'twixt my toes and a small fire to cook crabs over. Then shall I whistle for a gentle wind to bring the boats safe home.'

'Sand? Crabs? Whistling? What are you talking about?'

Lil frowned and touched her bruise. She suddenly felt light-headed and took a few deep breaths to steady herself.

'Are you sickening for something?' her mother asked. 'I could find a charm for that.'

Lil shook her head. The strange dizzy sensation had passed. She glanced down the steps and spotted Verne waiting below. Waving, she took Sally to join him and they started to walk towards Lil's home.

'How'd it go with the telly bloke?' the boy asked.

'Was a bit of a clotpole, but it was fine. Mum kept banging on about the shop though.'

'That vid you sent me was beyond amazing. I told you it was the zombie apocalypse. I'd have freaked if that thing came at me!'

'Well, maybe I was a bit frightened,' she confessed. 'Just a tiny bit. OK – loads. And so was Sal. The worst part was the wind blowing through its mouth right into mine – yeurgh! And don't tell Mum or Dad, cos they'll only make a huge fuss, but I think I was out cold for a few minutes. Had the weirdest dream. At least, I think I did. Can't really remember.'

'So are there any bones still lying about?' Verne asked ghoulishly. 'Can I see?'

Lil shrugged. 'I think they've taken them away now. They were just mucky old sticks and lumps – nothing special.'

'The thing that flew at you was!' he cried. 'That skull was horrible – looked like it was deliberately coming to get you!'

Lil laughed. 'You're as bad as my mother, with her doom-mongering. She laid it on real thick for the telly just now. Gave them the whole witchy works, she did.'

'Well, it creeped me out. It was evil!'

'Just bones, Verne. The very old, long-buried bones of someone who croaked hundreds of years ago.'

Verne laughed. 'You crack me up. You don't believe in anything. I mean, there's your folks being all hocus-pocus with their amazing shop, and you won't even give it the time of day when it comes flying through your bedroom window!'

'One more time, Verne – no such thing as magic. It doesn't exist, full stop. Why do you keep banging on about it?'

'Because it's exciting,' he said honestly. 'OK, maybe it's not magic, but aren't you even a bit curious as to who the skeleton was? All those years ago it was a living person, someone's dad or brother or . . .'

'No,' Lil said sharply. 'It was a woman.'

'How'd you know that?'

'I . . . I dunno. The long hair, I suppose.'

'They all had long hair in those days, didn't they? Or was it wigs?'

Lil raised her face and looked down Henrietta Street, towards the end row of cottages where she lived.

'It was a woman,' she muttered, her fingers touching a necklace Verne hadn't seen her wear before. It was made of three ammonites threaded on a grubby string. 'A young woman, full of rage and bitterness.'

'Just old bones you said!' he reminded her with a laugh. 'Well, hurry up, maybe they missed some.'

Before they could approach the cottage, a tall, slim man with receding hair and a square beard came out to meet them. It was Lil's father and he was dressed almost as eccentrically as his wife, with his rectangular pale-green-tinted spectacles, crisp linen granddad shirt and a waistcoat of dark blue silk.

'Can we get back in now?' Lil asked him. 'Verne wants to get his school books.'

'Not yet,' Mike Wilson said. 'The council guys are still checking for structural damage and making sure it's safe. But listen, last night – you did leave straightaway, didn't you? You didn't, er, move anything?'

'Such as? No, I got out of there fast as I could.'

'And you didn't see anyone hanging around? You locked the door after you?'

'What's this about?'

'If there was something else, you'd tell me, wouldn't you? This isn't a game, Lil, it's very serious. It isn't a toy, not like the resin replicas we sell. Do you understand?'

'I don't know what you're talking about.'

'They've looked everywhere,' her father said, frowning. 'It isn't where you said it was.'

'*What* isn't?'

'The thing that crashed into your room last night.'

'What? You saw the vid, Dad. I wasn't dreaming it!'

'Oh, the skeleton was there all right,' her father said. 'They've taken that away.'

'Then what are you going on about?'

'They've taken the *body* away, Lil. But the head . . . they can't find the head. The skull has disappeared.'

4

Lil and Verne took Sally down to Tate Hill Sands. The Westie was off the lead and ambling slowly, investigating the many varied smells of the beach. The storm had left behind clumps of glistening seaweed and great chunks of driftwood. The two friends were still discussing the mystery of the missing skull.

'Maybe someone broke in?' Verne suggested, kicking up the soft sand.

'The skeleton had already done that!' Lil answered. 'Besides, what would a burglar want with it? Why not take the telly or something valuable? There were plenty of other skulls just lying about in the gardens if that's what they really wanted.'

'It's going to be all over school on Monday. They already think you're weird; now they'll call you a grave robber, stealing body parts for evil magic.'

'Casting spells using dead bodies is necromancy,' Lil said. 'White witches don't do that.'

'Tracy and her gang don't care about facts. They want you to be making potions out of baby fat and eating bats. They'll probably say you caused the whole thing in the first place. You saw how scared they were of you yesterday.'

'If they're dumb enough to believe in that codswallop, they deserve to be scared.'

'I believe in it.'

'Well, you're bonkers. I don't scare you, do I?'

'Nah, we've known each other since we were in nappies.'

'Mine were black. I've seen the photos – and my dummy had plastic fangs!'

'Ha – brilliant.'

'You were the only kid who didn't scream when I turned up at your parties and the only one who ever came to mine.'

'I've always loved going to your house. It's full of fantastic things.'

Lil smiled.

'Witchy tat and way too many sepia prints of Victorian Whitby,' she said. Then added, 'Verne, you don't believe I took that manky head, do you?'

'Course not.'

'Thank you.'

'It would be a cool thing to have though.'

'Don't be weird.'

They had walked to the water's edge and followed

it round to where the sand gave way to dark grey rocks. The beach was deserted except for a solitary figure sitting on one of the largest boulders, gazing out to sea, leisurely casting daffodils on to the gently lapping waters.

She was slender and dressed in garish, clashing colours, topped off with a long lime green wig. It was unmistakably Cherry Cerise.

'I forgot to tell you!' Verne whispered. 'I saw her last night. She'd tied herself to the bridge and was singing and flapping her arms about. She's an absolute flake.'

Lil regarded the woman with new interest. Cherry Cerise was another of Whitby's eccentric oddities. She kept herself to herself and her odd appearance and abrupt manner were enough to keep the nosiest at bay.

'She does dress loopy,' Lil said. 'But then look at us Wilsons.'

'Yeah, but your mum and dad are witches and they're walking adverts for the shop. Makes perfect sense. She just looks like a rainbow threw up on her. She was waving torches around last night you know.'

'Torches?'

'There were coloured lights anyway. She was shining them into the wind. Crazy!'

'I think she looks fun.'

The thin woman turned her head towards them

and her mouth twisted with displeasure when she saw the two children staring at her.

Throwing the last daffodil on to the water, she left the rock and went striding past, enormous sunglasses firmly on her nose and bangles and bracelets clattering at her wrists.

'Can't go anywhere in this town no more without bumping into ungroovy goths every way you turn!' she snarled. 'Place is infested with them. Like rats or roaches in capes. Lords save me from mass melancholia and universal drabness!'

'Told you she was a dingbat,' Verne said with a chuckle. 'I don't think she even recognised me from last night. Mind you, she had sunglasses on then as well.'

'She's got a point about the clothes,' Lil said. 'I never want to wear black ever again. Listen, I've been working on a grand plan.'

'What sort of plan?'

'Can't tell you yet. But I'm going to wake this miserable town up and bring some colour to it.'

'How'd you mean? Is it a secret? You know I can keep them.'

'I know, but . . . I want to see if it's doable. I've already made a good start, and I'm ready to put phase one into action so you'll find out very soon.'

'Don't say you've got a secret until you're ready to spill. That's really aggravating. You –'

Verne cut himself off as he realised the time. He'd been away from the arcade much longer than he'd said.

'Got to go! Clarke will kill me. Listen, can you come round later with my books? We can go through that homework.'

Lil looked evasive. 'Sorry,' she said. 'I'll see if Mum or Dad can bring them. I've got to get my room sorted – unless I've been arrested for skull rustling. And Sal really needs a bath, plus I want to carry on with my secret project.'

'You're very annoying today,' he told her.

Lil looked around. 'Hang on, where is Sal?'

Verne glanced back down the beach, but there was no sign of her and it was no use calling her name.

They split up. Lil ran over the sand to see if Sally was heading for home and Verne made his way round the base of the cliff, searching behind the rocks.

Presently he shouted, 'She's here!'

Sally was by the edge of a small pool, pawing at something gingerly and giving it dubious sniffs.

Verne tapped her gently, to get her attention.

'Dead crab?' the boy said. 'You'll be sick if you eat that . . .'

His expression changed. It wasn't a crab at all. Sally had discovered the skeletal remains of a human hand – yet another gruesome relic torn from the cliff high above by the storm.

It was black with age and parchment-like skin was shrivelled over the bones. The fingers were clenched round what appeared to be a large clod of mud, but Sally's curious paws had scored little trenches into it. Verne's eyes widened when he saw glimpses of gleaming gold.

He reached down and scraped more of the mud away. The revealed gold reflected the sunlight up into his eyes. Verne caught his breath and took the strange find in his hands. What could it be?

'She all right?' Lil called, approaching.

Verne started and, for some reason he couldn't explain, furtively slipped the severed hand and whatever it was holding into his rucksack.

'Yes,' he answered, a little flustered. 'She's fine. Panic over.'

Sally's tail wagged when Lil stooped to stroke her head. Then the dog turned her good eye to Verne, expecting him to show what she had been clever enough to find.

'I really have to go,' the boy said instead.

'We'll walk with you to the road,' Lil offered.

'No time. Got to race back.'

And he darted off, with the macabre discovery stowed safely in his rucksack.

When Verne reached the amusement arcade, he found Clarke and his girlfriend Amy both squashed into the change booth. They didn't seem to mind how late he was and seemed almost disappointed to leave.

Verne spent the next hour unable to concentrate on anything other than the mysterious object Sally had discovered. He was desperate to take it out of his rucksack and examine it closely. Five times he dispensed the wrong change and he was too distracted to take much notice of the customers who complained. He didn't understand why he had hidden it from Lil. Perhaps it was because she was being secretive herself and he wanted a secret of his own.

When his mother finally arrived to take over, he hurried out of the back of the arcade, ran up a flight of metal stairs and let himself into their home. The Thistlewoods lived on the building's top two floors.

Thinking he was alone, Verne nearly jumped out of his skin when he ran into a tall figure in the hall. It was his father's steampunk costume for the approaching Goth Weekend, hanging from the banister – a Victorian robot butler made from a leather tailcoat, overlaid with copper tubing. The face was an adapted hockey mask, with old torch lenses for eyes and a brass tea-strainer for the mouth. It was the first time Verne had seen it fitted together and it was very impressive. Taking a firmer grip on the straps of his rucksack, he started to go upstairs.

'That you, Verne?' a voice called out from the living room.

'Yes!' he answered.

'Give us a hand, will you?'

The boy froze, wondering if his dad somehow knew what he was sneaking into the house. Turning back, Verne stuck his head round the door, feeling guilty.

He needn't have worried. His father was kneeling by a large wooden cabinet, peering into an open panel beneath the glass front. It was a vintage, coin-operated automaton from the 1930s. There was a collection of these old amusements in one corner of the arcade and they were still popular with the tourists. For one old penny, purchased for twenty pence at the change booth, the motor inside made crudely carved figures judder into life and act out a scenario with basic jerky movements. The themes were either morbid or humorous. There was a haunted house, an execution with an axe, a gruesome mortuary, the hallucinations of a drunkard and one of a newly-wed couple that transformed into a henpecked husband and his rolling pin-wielding wife. Verne liked the morbid ones best.

The automaton Verne's father had brought upstairs into the apartment, and was currently examining, depicted an American execution by electric chair. It hadn't worked for years and Dennis Thistlewood was often tinkering with it.

'I'm trying to fit that motor I got off eBay,' he told his son. 'Could do with some help; make sure I don't lose any vital bits.'

Normally, Verne would have leaped at the chance. He loved those old automata and had always wanted to see this one in action. The head of the condemned prisoner was supposed to light up when the fatal moment came. But today the boy was impatient to get away.

'You know I'm useless at that, Dad,' he said.

'OK, Klumsythumbs,' Mr Thistlewood said, using the name Verne had called himself due to various botched attempts at repairs in the past. 'So what do you think of Mr Potts?'

'Who?'

'That's what I've called my robot butler outfit. Looks good, doesn't he?'

'Why Mr Potts?' Verne asked, recognising the twinkle in his father's eye that usually preceded a terrible joke.

'First name Jack,' Dennis said with a chuckle and an emphatic wink. 'Jack Potts, get it? Because we own an arcade . . .'

Verne groaned loudly and headed for the door, leaving his father sniggering, head stuck back inside the cabinet, tapping connections and scratching his chin with a screwdriver.

Rushing upstairs, Verne closed his bedroom door and drew the severed hand from his rucksack, placing it on his desk. Catching his breath, he gazed at the artefact in fascination. It was a right hand, most

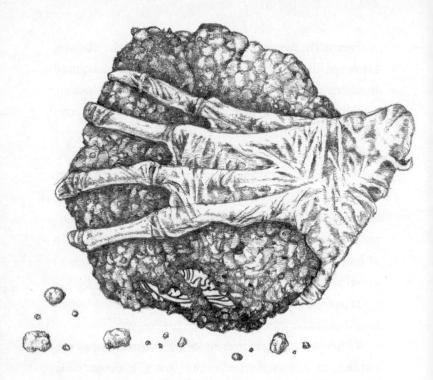

likely a man's judging by the size. From the state of
the bones, he guessed that the wrist had been hacked
through long ago. It hadn't snapped off last night. It
must have been buried like this and had lain in the
ground for hundreds of years.

Verne placed his own hand next to it. How small
it was in comparison. The guilt kicked in again – he
knew he shouldn't have taken it. It wasn't too late; he
could return it to the beach now and no one would
ever know what he had done. But the blackened
bones exerted a curious power over him, so he didn't
move and continued to sit and stare.

Carefully, he touched the withered skin. It was hard as old leather. He wondered again what that dead hand was holding. The fingers were locked firmly in position and Verne had to prise them open. Three of them snapped like twigs and broke off.

The boy didn't seem to notice or care. He lifted the muddy clump from the dead palm and weighed it in his own. It was unusually heavy for its size. Where he had scraped the soil away, the glitter of gold danced across his eyes.

Hastily, he pulled a T-shirt from a drawer and wiped the rest of the mud clear. Then he gazed down at the wondrous treasure in astonishment.

'Oh wow . . .' he murmured. 'Just wow.'

At first he thought it was an old-fashioned pocket watch, but it was shaped more like a hazelnut and was too big to squeeze into a waistcoat pocket. There was no winder visible either and no loop to fasten it to a chain. It appeared to be made entirely from gold that was as bright as the day it entered the ground.

Verne's fingertips stroked the cold surface. It was more beautiful and intricately patterned than anything he had ever seen. The graveyard mould of centuries was embedded in grooves round the strange symbols etched across the surface and Verne was thrilled to discover that many sank down and clicked back up when he pushed. Others looked as though they might swivel across or twist, but there was too much dirt blocking the movement and he didn't want to force a delicate mechanism or break a hidden spring.

Marvelling, he searched for a catch that would flip the front open. It was obviously an extremely valuable trinket or scientific instrument of some sort, but what? He had no idea. Perhaps it wasn't supposed to open. There was no obvious split down the middle.

Putting it to his ear, he shook it gently. It didn't rattle. If there were any clockwork parts inside, they weren't loose. A few crumbs of soil dropped out.

Verne turned it over and examined it more closely. He recognised some of the designs from books and items in the Wilsons' shop. This meant one thing to him – they must be magical!

Then he noticed, running between the crowded symbols, a scrolling banner, engraved with a single word.

Verne carried the precious object over to his computer and began to search the web. He quickly found that the word was Latin, but was still puzzled when he read what it meant.

'Beyond measure.'

Putting the device in front of his keyboard, he shook his head, perplexed.

'What the heck are you?' he murmured.

5

When Lil got home, her bedroom was still in a terrible state. There was mud and broken glass everywhere.

With the help of her father, she sponged down every surface and the carpet was taken up and thrown out. Sally made herself comfortable on the settee downstairs and kept out of the way, her good eye watching the TV they switched on for her.

The one thing that dismayed Lil was the discovery that her Lucky Duck, a small glass ornament from the local Whitby glassworks, had been smashed. Her late grandmother had bought it for her on the day she was born and, in spite of her scorn for all things superstitious, she couldn't help feeling that perhaps this was a bad omen.

When Mrs Wilson closed the shop and returned home, her daughter and husband were still busy. She joined in with the cleaning and by eight o'clock it was finally ready, with a rug on the bare boards as a temporary measure until they could redecorate.

After a takeaway supper of fish and chips, Lil decided to have an early night and went to bed, taking Sally with her. The little dog was very content, having eaten battered fish skin as a treat.

Lil opened the door and snapped on the light. It didn't feel like her room any more. The bare floorboards gave it a strange echo and she wasn't sure she'd ever feel safe in there again. Her nose wrinkled. Mrs Wilson had done as she promised and performed a purification ritual to banish evil forces and the pungent smell of the incense she had burned still lingered. Lil's mum had also brought a Nightmarechaser from the shop to hang on the wall. It was a mad, witchy invention of her own, a more proactive form of Dreamcatcher, being a hideous thing with bird skulls, small bells, black feathers and dangling bottles containing herbs and powders.

Lil placed Sally on the end of the bed and the Westie curled up on the freshly washed fleece blanket, tucking her face into her paws.

The girl spent some minutes packing a large rucksack with items from her knitting bag. Then she turned off the light and got into bed, fully dressed

except for her shoes. Checking her phone, she was surprised there were no messages from Verne. She had been too secretive today, he hadn't liked that and Lil felt bad about it. She hoped he'd forgive her tomorrow when he saw what she'd done. It would be easier to explain it then anyway; she hadn't known how to put it into words – she knew it would have sounded totally stupid. She just hoped he'd understand.

Setting the alarm, she tucked the phone down one of her socks. Then she lay her head on a new pillow and the exertions of the day caught up with her. In spite of her excitement, she was soon fast asleep.

Across the river, Bev and Angie had been summoned to Tracy's house and were now slumped on the settee in the front room. Earlier that evening, Tracy had rowed with her boyfriend after they had watched Lil on the news and he had made the massive mistake of saying he thought the Wilson girl was brave and cool. Angie and Bev listened sympathetically as Tracy griped about him and what she'd like to do to that freaky Lil Wilson.

'It's not brave to stand in front of a window as skeletons come smashing through it,' Tracy vented. 'It's moronic.'

'She's well weird though,' Bev said. 'I wouldn't mess with her.'

'A dead body went right for her like a heat-seekin' missile,' Angie agreed, grimacing. 'That ain't normal. It didn't happen to anyone else in her street, did it?'

Tracy's anger at her boyfriend made her forget the fear she had felt yesterday on the pier.

'Rubbish!' she snapped. 'There's nothing spooky about the Wilsons. They're just mental.'

Her friends twisted their mouths and looked uncomfortable. In the corner of the room, Eggs and Bacon – two hamsters that belonged to Tracy's young brother – were scurrying around the plastic tubes of their futuristic habitat, making enough noise to be a distracting nuisance.

'What's got into them?' Bev asked.

'They're nocturnal,' Tracy said, sneering in their direction. 'Our Liam used to have them in his room, but they kept him awake all night. Not usually this rowdy though. Shut up over there!'

'It's well wrong, only comin' out at night,' said Angie, pulling a face.

'They're just rats without tails,' Bev added.

'Do you think them Wilsons keep rats? It's the sort of mingin' thing they'd do. Bet their house is proper rank.'

Tracy gave an exasperated grunt.

'Stop going on about them!' she said. 'They're nothin' special. Anyone can pretend to be witchy and ponce about in cloaks being a prat. It's all a con for their tatty junk shop. Look, I'll show you. Shift those mags off the coffee table and sit round it.'

The girls obeyed while Tracy took a glass tumbler from her dad's drinks cabinet and ripped some pages from a notepad. Bev raised her eyebrows at Angie as Tracy scribbled hastily on the paper and tore it into small squares.

'What you doin'?' Bev asked.

Tracy grinned back at her and started arranging the paper scraps in a circle on the table. She had written a letter on each piece and 'Yes' and 'No' on

two larger bits which she placed on opposite sides. Then she turned the tumbler upside down in the centre.

'Put your fingertips on it,' she told the other two. 'We're goin' to have a seance. We're gonna speak to the spirits of the dead . . . wooooooh. How's that for cool and brave?'

'I don't want to,' Bev said, leaning away. 'You shouldn't mess with that sort of thing.'

Angie agreed with her and, if the frenzied racket coming from the hamster cage was anything to go by, so did Eggs and Bacon.

'Shut it!' Tracy bawled but the hamsters continued to dart round the coloured tubes.

'They would drive me nuts,' Bev declared. 'They having fits or what?'

'Ignore them,' Tracy ordered. 'Now put your fingers on the glass!' She looked so fierce the other girls didn't dare disobey.

Tracy took a deep breath and gazed up at the ceiling.

'Is there anybody there?' she asked in a haunted warble.

The glass slid across the table to 'Yes'.

'You pushed it,' Bev accused her.

'Never!' Tracy lied.

'This is too creepy for me,' Angie put in.

'What do you want to tell us, spirit?' Tracy continued.

The glass began to move again, visiting one letter after another.

'What's it doin'?' Angie asked.

'Spellin' out a message,' Bev told her.

L-I-L I-S U-G-L-Y

The girls fell about laughing. When they recovered another message came through straight away.

W-I-L-S-O-N S-T-I-N-X

They laughed some more.

'Does Lil Wilson ever wash?' Tracy asked.

NO the glass declared immediately.

'My turn!' Angie insisted.

W-E R H-O-T-T-A

U R B-E-S-T E-V-A

T-R-U

Still laughing, they jostled for control of the tumbler, trying to think of even funnier messages. In the corner of the room, the hamsters stopped running around their cage and began frantically clawing at the plastic walls. Overhead, the light bulb crackled.

For some moments, the room flickered in and out of darkness. The girls squealed.

'Now *that's* spooky!' Tracy declared.

The other two giggled nervously. Bev shivered.

'Gone cold in here,' she said.

'Quiet too,' Angie added. The hamsters had retreated into their straw nest and were silent.

The glass began to move under their fingers again.

I A-M W-A-T-C-H-I-N-G Y-O-U

'Err . . . what?' Tracy asked. 'Which one of you did that?'

Bev and Angie shook their heads. The glass slid across to the letters once more.

I W-I-L-L B-E W-I-T-H Y-O-U S-O-O-N

'Stop doin' that,' Angie said. 'It's not funny or nothin'.'

'Weren't me,' Bev told her.

'Me either,' Tracy swore.

Y-O-U H-A-V-E P-R-E-T-T-Y N-E-C-K-S

Angie took her finger off the glass and folded her arms. 'Stupid game!' she snorted. 'I'm not playin' no more.'

'Me neither,' said Bev, doing the same.

With only Tracy's finger on it, the glass began to glide across to another letter.

D

'See!' Angie cried. 'It *is* you!'

A

'It really isn't!' Tracy answered, pulling her finger clear.

The tumbler's movements ceased.

'Oh yeah?' Bev said. 'Who then?'

Before Tracy could reply, the glass began to move again. Without anyone touching it, the tumbler slid round the polished table by itself.

R-K

Suddenly the paper letters flew up into their faces. The girls shrieked and ran from the room. The glass shot off the table and smashed against the wall. In the hallway, as Bev and Angie continued to scream, Tracy paused and caught her breath when she realised she wasn't remotely afraid; in fact, she felt excited and vibrantly alive.

'DARK,' she murmured to herself, repeating the final word.

Night deepened over Whitby. Pubs emptied and stumbling footsteps clumped home through the narrow streets. The lights around the church and the abbey went out, engulfing the East Cliff in gloom. On both sides of the river, cheery windows winked to black and boats in the harbour looked like they were bobbing on ink. Midnight ticked by and eventually there were no sounds other than the lapping water.

Above the Thistlewoods' amusement arcade, Verne

slept with the mysterious treasure he had found tucked under his pillow. He had hidden the fragments of the severed hand in a drawer and had spent most of the evening admiring and examining the Nimius, cleaning out the fine grooves with an old toothbrush and polishing it with a soft cloth. He still had no idea what it could possibly be, but he knew it must be very valuable and felt like the worst sort of thief. Several times as he rubbed it he had felt the object twist and click, and each time he stared at it in anticipation. But nothing further happened; it didn't start ticking or opening, and when he looked closer he couldn't even work out how it could have twisted. It certainly didn't budge when he tried to move it himself. And so he hid it under the pillow, wondering if the morning would deliver up any fresh answers and whether he should confess and hand it in.

That night the boy's dreams were filled with glittering images of the strange symbols that crowded the surface of his precious find. They whirled through his sleep accompanied by the steady movement of giant cogs, ratchet wheels, levers, slender springs and pendulums. A shining liquid pulsed through snaking glass tubes and an emerald flame burned within a revolving diamond. But the shadow of Verne's guilt was always present, flooding his dreams with darkness.

'Nimius,' a distant, commanding voice echoed.

'Deliver unto me the Nimius . . . This time Scaur Annie shall not win.'

Verne mumbled unhappily. He had a sensation of falling, spinning down through the intricate golden mechanisms. Next moment his eyes snapped open and he lurched forward. He was no longer in his bedroom, but striding into Whitby's only inn, The White Horse.

'Vittles is ready when you are, my Lord Pyke,' George Sneaton the fat innkeeper greeted him, nodding deferentially. 'Why, Annie!' he added when he saw the soot-smeared girl wrapped in the noble's cloak. 'Whatever's happened to you?'

'Sandsend folk and a preacher,' she answered fiercely. 'They burned my hut and wanted to burn me too.'

'Fetch ale for her,' Melchior Pyke ordered. 'And bring the supper at once; this girl is almost blue with cold and shock.'

'Right you are, my lord,' the innkeeper said, casting a concerned glance at Annie before rushing into the kitchen.

Melchior Pyke led the girl upstairs to the private parlour set aside for him and guided her to a padded leather chair near the fireplace.

'You're trembling like a lotus petal in the rains,' he told her. 'That's not to be wondered at; you've suffered much this night at the hands of that accursed Puritan.'

Still huddled in his cloak, Scaur Annie peered around her. She was not accustomed to sitting in a proper chair and she took in the surrounding luxury with curious eyes. There were real candles in the tin sconces, not mere rushlights, and the fire irons were twisted and curled ornately. On one panelled wall there was even a small looking-glass, a rare object she had never seen before. She had only ever encountered her reflection in rock pools and she wondered if her face looked different when undisturbed by ripples. On a long table beneath it was an impressive collection of books and some unusual brass objects, the functions of which she could not begin to guess at. But what captivated her attention most was a painting over the mantle of the infant Christ in the Virgin Mary's arms. Annie stared long at it.

Kneeling beside her, Melchior Pyke dabbed at the burns on her arms with a wet cloth. Annie flinched and pulled away.

'Peace, little sand sprite,' he said soothingly. 'Your hurts need tending and must be cleansed else they'll fester.'

'I know what to do,' she answered proudly. 'I'm the cure-all for the poor folk hereabouts. I've got salves that heal and take the sting away.'

'Not any more you haven't,' he reminded her.

The girl relented and let him wash the burns on her arms and shoulder. The tenderness of his touch surprised her. No man had ever shown her such kindness. While he was absorbed in his careful ministrations, she took the opportunity to get a good look at her saviour. His face was handsome and bronzed by travels in hot, distant lands. She had heard the gossiping fishwives talk of how this fancy nobleman had charmed the town with his smooth words and crinkling smile, and Annie found herself liking him too.

He raised his eyes suddenly. Annie averted her own and stared back at the Madonna above the fireplace. She could feel her face reddening, but hoped the grime and soot concealed it.

'A bairn with its mam,' she said at length, still enchanted by the painting. 'That's fair pretty and clever done. She's full of the strongest love there is. She'll do owt for that precious mite, guard it close, keep every danger away, take all harms to herself to save it, at the price of her own sweet life.'

Melchior Pyke rose to his feet and handed her the cloth. 'Here, mistress, the flames did not lick deep; keep the wounds clean and healing will be swift.'

He gave the painting another glance. 'You see more than I do in this. It smacks too much of Rome for my taste.'

The girl hugged her shoulders.

'My folks was carried off when plague come to Whitby,' she said quietly. 'The same year as old Queen Bess died.'

'Then that was a sad time for us both. My tutor and mentor, William Gilberd, died in the November. He set me square upon the long road of learning. He was the Queen's physician and much more besides: astronomer, scholar of natural philosophy . . .'

He gestured towards one of the books on the table. 'I keep his great work, *De Magnete*, by me wherever I travel. His passing grieved me, though I was a lad of fifteen summers and still had kin, yet you would not have been much more than a nursling when you were orphaned.'

'Right enough. But I were lucky; I was took in and cared for.'

'It is heartening to know the Church can still be charitable.'

'Weren't no church!' the girl said with a snort, followed quickly by the ghost of a smile. 'I've got no love for that and only go Sundays so I don't get fined. No, my mam had friends, special secret friends. Was them as kept me safe. They –'

She broke off and began to cough, blaming the smoke in her lungs, but Melchior Pyke guessed it was because she felt she had said too much.

'Where is that oafish innkeeper?' he declared, turning to his manservant who was skulking in the doorway. 'Mister Dark, hurry those victuals and make sure it's the finest October ale for our guest, not his usual insipid brew. Then scare up the innkeeper's daughter and send her here. Somewhere under this roof there must be fitting garments to be had.'

The manservant lingered a moment, his eyes staring past his master at the huddled girl. She had begun washing her face in the basin and the splashing water caught the firelight. The droplets were bright as burning diamonds. His scarred lips twisted more unpleasantly than usual and his brows bunched together.

'She has a pretty neck,' he said.

'Every neck is prettier than yours,' Melchior Pyke told him. 'Now stop gaping and do as I've bidden.'

Mister Dark gave him a surly glance, then departed.

'Ain't no one likes him around here,' Annie stated as she wiped her face with the cloth.

'You must not mind Mister Dark,' Melchior Pyke assured her. 'His looks are against him, but he has his uses.'

'Ain't his face,' Annie replied, with a shake of her head. 'That don't matter. It's what's inside that counts for everything. But there's a force in him that makes the air thick as the threat of storm. Makes hackles rise and sets dogs to howling. Goose skin pricks out whenever he's close.'

The noble was taken aback by her words. He

was accustomed to people judging his servant on appearance alone. This girl had insight and a keen intelligence.

Scaur Annie did not notice his admiring gaze. Her eyes had been drawn to a delicate gilt arrow balanced on a needle, over by the books. It had started to swing wildly the instant Mister Dark left the room to go stomping down the stairs beyond.

She touched the three ammonites around her neck as if for protection.

'Even yon dainty play arrow wagged when he went,' she said.

Melchior Pyke looked at the instrument she pointed at.

'That is a versorium,' he informed her. 'It detects the presence of a mysterious, invisible power called electricus. Mister Dark is brimming over with it because that is how he was revived on our first meeting.'

'What do that mean?'

'When I first encountered Mister Dark, he was swinging from a gallows, hence the condition of his unfortunate neck. I thought he was dead as a stone and he should have been; he had been hanging there all day. I needed a cadaver to further my studies, so I cut him down and took him back to my workshop.'

'Dead shouldn't be mucked with,' Annie said

crossly. 'Goes against all that's proper that does.'

Melchior Pyke chuckled at her outrage. 'As you have seen, he was not dead. Somehow an atom of life must have lingered. When I began my first experiment, summoning that electricus force with a contrivance of my own devising, the remaining gasp in him was jolted into a sudden and desperate inhalation and I realised, to my great wonderment, that the man was alive.

'"Dark! Dark!" he shrieked as he convulsed and kicked upon the slab. "Naught but dark!" And that is how I named him, for he has no memory of his existence before the noose, nor even what crime he had committed to warrant the drop. His mind had been washed clear. Electricus is a marvellous enigma; we do not yet know all its virtues and caprices. But the residue is still within him. He can cause tiny sparks of blue fire to leap from his fingers. I will get him to demonstrate when he returns. The King of Bohemia and the Mughal Emperor have admired and been amazed by that singular talent.'

'I don't want to see it,' she said vehemently. 'You did a foul deed cutting him down and setting a power in him he never ought to have owned.'

'Skimble-skamble superstition!' he answered. 'Mister Dark has been in my service these seven years and I've never known a more loyal servant. The fellow is uncommon clever too and has been of great assistance with my experiments. His blanched mind was a sponge for learning and he has the strength of five hale men.'

'Nay,' Annie said. 'You call it what you will. There's a cold winter in him, a dead badness. Dark be his name and darker still be his nature. Your man has wandered evil paths and you don't know what's hiding in his heart. There ain't a squeeze of good in his soul – if he's still got one. If he serves anyone, it ain't you.'

'You're beginning to sound like that ignorant Puritan.'

Annie spat in the fire. 'John Ashe were right about one thing,' she said. 'Your man do prowl about the shore and cliffs at night when goodly bodies ought to be abed. Most times he ain't alone neither. He got some owl or tame bat or summat. I seen them together, a way off – and seen him at other times, on his own, watching and spying on me.'

'And what are *you* doing, roaming through the night? Aren't you a goodly body?'

Annie shrugged.

'Looking for them plants what only flower under the moon,' she answered. 'And them things what don't crawl or creep under the sun.'

'For what possible purpose?'

The firelight danced in her eyes and she let out a gurgle of laughter. 'It were two things John Ashe were right about,' she confessed. 'Scaur Annie *is* a witch, like her mam before her.'

Before he could comment, the innkeeper's daughter, Mary Sneaton, came bustling in, carrying a mutton pie, a loaf and a jug of ale. Behind her, more sullen than usual, was Mister Dark. He was draped in an assortment of Mary's old gowns and shifts that she had thrust at him hastily and he wasn't amused. She was a dumpy, scurrying type of woman, several years older than Annie, and kept the tipplers of the public bar in order with sharp words and a ready clout.

'Now out you go, m'lord,' she shooed, 'whilst Annie attires herself. This isn't a bawdy house; 'tweren't seemly for you to bathe her naked arms and legs.'

Laughing, Melchior Pyke left the room along with his manservant.

'Yon lordship is a true gallant and double handsome with it,' Mary told Annie as she gathered the extra fabric of her old kirtle in pleats round the young witch's slender waist and began securing them with pins. 'But you have to think of your reputation.'

Annie shrugged and took a swig of ale. 'There's plenty who already reckon I'm worse than I am!' she said.

'Not here in Whitby there aren't, so don't you go giving idle tongues cause to doubt it. There's a dry attic here with a cot you can make use of till you gets fixed. But beware that manservant. He's a vile fartleberry and has the very devil of a temper when drunk. He's fallen foul of everyone and Father won't serve him no more, or suffer him to sleep under our roof, so he beds down in the outbuilding. I don't know how his lordship stomachs his company. I can't abide the way he stares at me, hungry like. Gives me the shudders. The horses don't like sight nor smell of him neither, or we'd have put him in the stables.'

'Animals have sense,' Annie said.

'Even our cat, the big one we called Catesby because he was always lurking in the cellars, like that traitor with the gunpowder, he disappeared the very first night they arrived and hasn't been seen since. Best ratter we ever had, he was.'

Mary stood back.

'There,' she said, with pins in her mouth. 'How do that feel?'

Annie looked down at herself. She'd never worn anything before that didn't have holes in it.

'I feels like the Queen of the whole North Riding!' she declared.

'It's a poor royal majesty who has such a tangled rook's nest on top of her head. Come look at yourself in the glass.'

Annie stepped over to the mirror and gazed at her reflection. She was astonished to see her face so sharp and clear for the first time and almost jumped aside in alarm.

'What cleverness,' she said. 'And no waving weeds or crab belches spoiling it. I like it better than rock pools.'

Her wonder was cut short as Mary tried to pull a comb through her hair.

'Oooowww!'

'Hold still and stop shrieking!'

'Owww! You'll rip my scalp clean off. Oowww!'

Annie swung round and slapped Mary across the face. Mary roared, drew back her hand and gave as good as she got. They crashed against the table, sending books and scientific instruments flying.

The door burst open and Melchior Pyke charged inside.

'Here's a merry dogfight to wager on!' he cried. 'My coin is on the wild stray; she looks accustomed to bloody knuckles. What say you, Mister Dark?'

The tall, gaunt man entered and grinned. His master stepped forward and dragged Scaur Annie clear of Mistress Sneaton.

'Yet I'll not have you turn my private room into a bear garden,' he said sternly. 'My books are worth more than your broken heads.'

Annie glared at him. A red handprint glowed angrily on her cheek and her hair was even more of a chaotic, matted snarl than ever, and now a comb was lodged in it.

'You keep it and make good use,' Mary told her,

storming out. 'I must be getting back to the public bar, else there'll be lewd songs ringing loud.'

Melchior Pyke grinned then turned back to a fuming Annie.

'Thou art more jester than witch,' he commented, regarding her appearance.

'That's all you know!' she replied hotly. 'I speak truly – and you, my fine, fancy lord, aren't in Whitby just for them reasons you pretended. You're up to mischief, you and that knot-necked servant. But mark what Scaur Annie tells thee now: you won't profit by it and, before all's done, you'll learn there's more to this world than what's in books. Aye, and much more in Whitby that you won't never know about, and if you did, your mind would break.'

'Do not presume to know the strength of my mind, mistress. I have beheld such things on my travels as would turn your tangled hair white. What would you know of the powers that dwell in forsaken temples beyond the edge of maps, or the dire knowledge contained within ancient writings?'

'There's more than all that in this here town. The cliffs keep deep, dark secrets, as old as can be.'

Melchior Pyke gave a disbelieving laugh. 'I've a mind to show you my real work here,' he told her. 'That would curb your empty boasts, to see a true miracle in the making. But no, for the moment it must remain hidden.'

'Annie was raised by miracles, my lord,' she answered.

'There are none to compare with the one created by Sir Melchior Pyke,' he declared. 'It will astound the world.'

'Astound the world!' Verne repeated in his sleep as his own familiar bedroom reappeared around him.

With his eyes closed, the boy rose from the bed, pulled on his dressing gown, reached under the pillow and went downstairs.

6

Across the river, in the Wilsons' cottage, Sally was snoring softly and Lil was also fast asleep. The old curtains had gone the way of the carpet and the new window was uncovered, but there was no moon. In the darkness, the mirror showed as an ellipse of pale silver on top of the dresser. Within the oval frame a shape was growing and it was not the reflection of something in the room. It came closer and closer until a foul, evil face pressed against the underside of the glass as if it was a window. It was the missing skull.

The hideous object angled round so the empty eye sockets could gaze at the sleeping girl. The jaw opened in a ghastly grin and the surface of the mirror began to ripple like water. As it shimmered, tendrils of hair came bleeding through, writhing like seaweed under the waves. They flowed into the bedroom, followed by the head.

Floating out of the mirror, the skull rose above the dresser, hair seething, and began to drift across the room.

On the window sill, the two herb pouches that Mrs Wilson had placed there to ward off dark forces began to tremble. The dried agrimony they contained smouldered and a thread of smoke curled up through the cloth. Above the headboard, the Nightmarechaser twitched and its black feathers scraped the wall. The powder inside the small glass phials sparkled and burned and the bells tinkled, but Lil remained sound asleep and Sally could not hear them. As the skull approached, the Nightmarechaser jiggled wildly, yet it was no match for that advancing power. The hook worked free of the wall and the Nightmarechaser fell down behind the bed.

Lil shifted in her sleep and gave a small, unhappy murmur. The skull moved over the bedclothes to reach her upturned face. Poised above the girl's pillow, its empty eyes stared down and the jaw opened wider.

A hissing voice, filled with spite and malice, issued from the dead mouth.

'You are my vessel,' it snarled. 'Through you, I shall work my vengeance. Melchior Pyke can't never rise again. His miracle must stay hid.'

'Scaur Annie . . .' Lil breathed.

The skull hissed again and the writhing hair brushed across the girl's face.

It was a warm summer night and a calm lay over the sea. Annie was sitting on the moonlit shore, digging her toes in the sand and drawing swirls and circles around her.

At her side, gazing at the glimmering waters, was a strange, child-sized creature with large grey eyes and a nose like a shrivelled apple. Dried starfish were threaded in the loose mane of her long, shaggy hair and a string of shells and polished pebbles was around her neck. Her name was Nettie and she was an aufwader, one of the supernatural gnome-like people who lived inside the cliff.

'Speak to me of this man who has stolen you from us,' she said, her wrinkled face creasing with a gentle smile. 'We have seen you walking, arms entwined, over the cliffs. Hesper saw you kissing! Even old Esau has heard of it and his face grows the sourer daily. You know he has a liking for you.'

Annie continued drawing in the sand. 'Then we are the gossip of Whitby's every nook and corner,' she said. 'Up in the town and down in the caves of the fisherfolk. Are the hidden people as shocked as those whose tongues clack with displeasure above ground? 'Tis a great scandal – the ragged witch and her gentleman. John Ashe, the Puritan, believes I have bewitched my lord and denounces me to all who would listen. Even those I counted as friends now turn their faces as we pass.'

The aufwader reached out to clasp her hand.

'There is naught you could do to turn *our* hearts against you, dearest Annie,' she said earnestly. 'Your mother was my beloved friend and, when we took you

in, you captured our love completely.'

'Never was there a luckier child,' Annie said gratefully. 'In your caves there was no lack of lullabies or embraces.'

'Then be not angry if we worry overmuch. Have patience with our fussing and foolishness.'

Annie lifted her face and stared into the night. 'My gentleman is the star I must follow,' she answered simply. 'You should hear of the distant lands he has seen. I drink in every word. There is a rare delicacy, eaten by Arabian princes in the hottest desert: frozen snow flavoured with roses. Ain't that the most marvellous wonder? Melchior has promised I shall taste it one day.'

Nettie squeezed her hand. 'If he is truly the one for you, then you have my blessing,' she said.

'I love his very shadow,' Annie answered. 'And yet . . . there ain't total trust with us. I cannot tell him of you and the other fisherfolk, and he . . .'

Her voice trailed off and she dug at the sand impatiently.

'And he?' Nettie prompted. 'What does he not speak of? Is it his fearsome servant? Beware that creature, my little loveling.'

Annie shook her head. 'Mister Dark is a foul wretch, but he ain't the cloud between us.'

'Then what?'

'It is Melchior's great work. My gentleman will not say what keeps him so busy in the outbuildings of The White Horse. If he loved me as much as he swears, then why don't he show me? Why is it secret? What do he do in there?'

Nettie frowned at her.

'You must leave this jealous path,' she instructed. 'It will take you no place good. If you love him, then you must have faith. Trust is a delicate and hallowed thing;

once it is broken it can never be mended.'

Annie nodded and gave her a ready grin. 'You are right, of course, as ever,' she said brightly. 'I will bridle my curiosity and press him no more.'

Nettie hugged her.

'Will we see you tomorrow night?' she asked. 'All eyes will be looking for the Whitby witch. Please attend. I think Silas is going to ask Hesper to be his bride. I hope she says no; she would be too good a wife for him.'

'Another festival of the summer moon,' Annie reflected. 'How quick they come round each year. Aye, I shall be there.'

'For the feast – and the moon songs on the water after,' Nettie urged. 'You were always so excited to be in the boats when you was small.'

Annie nodded. The aufwader kissed her forehead, then hurried over the shore towards the rocks, disappearing in the shadows beneath the cliff.

Alone, Annie ceased digging in the sand and stared at the implement she had been using. It was a large iron key. She had stolen it that very afternoon.

'Just one brief glance within,' she told herself. 'None shall ever know and I won't never doubt him again.'

A short while later, Annie was standing barefoot in the stable yard of The White Horse inn. She glanced around uneasily. The moon cast deep, slanting shadows over the cold cobbles and Annie darted to the largest outbuilding. In a moment, the lock had been turned and she was inside.

The place was steeped in gloom, but a single lantern was hanging from one of the beams. By the dim light, Annie saw benches and tables laden with diverse tools, tall jars of coloured powders and cloudy liquids. Some of the larger jars contained preserved specimens of unusual animals from foreign lands. There was a small forge and iron crucibles. Charts and diagrams papered the walls. Weirdly shaped fragile glass vessels, connected by fine copper pipes, were ranged down one side of the room, and delicate brass instruments, scales and measures were neatly positioned along another. Magnifying lenses were angled over open books whose pages were crammed with exquisite and precise designs that meant nothing to Annie.

She gazed at everything in wonder, but still had no idea what Melchior was creating there.

As she roamed through the workshop, a pair of amber eyes shone down from the beams above.

Then, on a table all to itself, Annie saw a beautiful circular box, richly inlaid with exotic veneers, with a golden handle and standing on two feet carved like lion paws. She knew this had to be it. Smiling, she reached out her hand.

She was halted by a screeching wail and a terror flew down from the ceiling. Leathery wings beat in

Annie's face as a black-furred fiend with claws and glaring eyes hissed and snapped savagely at her neck.

She cried out and stumbled back, but the demon sank its talons into her bodice and bit her. Annie grabbed its neck and dragged it off, hurling it across the benches, smashing the bottles and jars in its way. The creature righted itself and flapped its large wings, ready to attack again.

Annie turned to flee, only to find Sir Melchior Pyke and Mister Dark standing in the doorway.

'Call it off,' Melchior told his manservant.

Mister Dark gave a shrill whistle. The creature made a mewling shriek and flew to his shoulder.

Annie stared in horror.

The creature arched its back, glowering murderously and dragging its claws through the leather of Mister Dark's jerkin. It was a large black cat, but one that had been surgically altered. Long scars were visible through the patchy fur where the great wings of a tropical bat had been sewn to its back. Mister Dark rubbed his thumb and forefinger together and bright blue sparks crackled about his hand. The horror pressed its head against his palm revealing four silver staples in its skull.

'What is that foul demon?' Annie cried.

'The alchemists of the east would call it a Takwin,' Melchior Pyke said. 'We simply call it Catesby. He is our most excellent watchdog, which is ironic, considering he used to be the inn's cat. Mister Dark took a fancy to the beast when we arrived and wanted to practise his needlework skills. We had a particularly fine example of a great golden bat in one of our jars and Mister Dark combined the two admirably. He's very adept with all things bloody. You'd think his big hands would be fit only for strangling horses, but they're remarkably dainty with fine tools.'

'It's as unnatural as him!'

'Unlovely they both may be,' he said, 'but at least they are loyal. What are you doing here, mistress? Was it your intent to rob me? Have you been playing me for a gull this whole time?'

'You think me a thief? No, my love!'

'And yet here you are, in a place forbidden, with a stolen key. What further proofs could there be for burglary? A justice would have no doubt of it.'

Annie shook her head desperately.

'I did but want to uncover your secret work, that I might know you better!' she swore. 'I desired only complete understanding between us.'

'Then why do you keep secrets from me?'

'I do not!'

'Are there not swathes of your life that you refuse to speak of? I have been honest in my dealings with you. Save for those questions that touched on my work, I have answered you with full and open frankness, because I have grown to love the Whitby witch. Yet your past is a mystery to me and you shine no light upon it, though we have spoken long about many matters. Who were those special folk who took you in after your parents died of plague? Why do you never talk of them? What are the deep mysteries about this town that you have hinted at? What are you hiding from me?'

Annie closed her eyes and shook her head. 'Those secrets ain't mine to share,' she said unhappily. 'I am the witch of Whitby, 'tis my sacred duty to keep certain things hid and safeguarded. Do not blame me for that.'

The nobleman looked hurt. 'Then I have been mistook and we have naught between us,' he told her sadly. 'Leave this place and do not seek me out again.'

Annie saw the pain in his eyes and knew she had wounded him. She could not bear it.

'Come up to the cliff with me,' she begged. 'This witch will break her oaths and tell you all.'

A deep purr began to vibrate in Catesby's throat and the electric sparks from Mister Dark's fingers glittered in its eyes.

Lil woke with a start. She was back in her bedroom and the phone was buzzing in her sock.

Sitting up, she removed the mobile and turned the alarm off. It was 3 a.m. Momentarily bemused, her thoughts were tangled with the shreds of an unpleasant dream about a winged cat that was already fading. Lil rubbed her forehead as the last traces evaporated and she was left with a peculiar hankering for rose-flavoured ice cream.

With bleary vision, she looked about her darkened room and shook the sleep from her head. Was the mirror moving, rippling like a small pool into which a stone had been dropped? Wiping her eyes, she stared again, and the mirror seemed to be its usual solid and unremarkable self.

Lil thought no more about it. She slipped from the bed and pulled on her trainers, twitching her nose at the bad smell in the room and wondering if she should give Sally a change of diet.

Taking a black cloak from the wardrobe, she fastened it round her neck. Then, with an affectionate glance back at the still sleeping Westie, she picked up her rucksack and stole from the room.

As silently as possible, she crept past her parents' bedroom, opened the child gate at the top of the stairs, put there to keep Sally safe, and closed it behind her. So far so good. Reaching the hall, she let herself out of the front door and stepped into Henrietta Street. It was a calm night without a breath of wind, and the scent of smouldering oak chippings, emanating from Fortune's kipper smokehouse nearby, threaded through the narrow ways of the East Cliff.

'Here we go,' she whispered to herself, glancing

left and right to make sure the street was deserted before setting off. 'Lil Wilson, yarn guerrilla, it's time to put your plan into action and start jazzing up this gloomy goth Mecca.'

Pulling the hood of her cloak over her head, she melted into the deep gloom beneath the huddled buildings and hurried towards the town.

An hour and a half later, Lil let herself back into the cottage. She had seen no one while she was out and was certain no one had seen her either, so she was feeling exhilarated. Grinning, she climbed the stairs and found Sally curled up behind the child gate. The little dog felt her footsteps through the floorboards and lifted her head to greet her.

'Oh, Sal,' Lil whispered, cupping the small, furry face in her hands. 'You shouldn't have jumped off the bed. You might've hurt yourself.'

Sally pawed her and wagged her tail in welcome. Any time away from Lil was too long. The girl picked her up and they returned to her room, where Lil settled her down on the bed.

'Mission accomplished, Sal,' she said softly. 'I was stealthy like a ninja and managed to put up every last piece. I can't wait for tomorrow to see what the reaction is!'

Still smiling, she gave Sally a treat, then pulled out her knitting bag, feeling too fired up to sleep.

Her needles were soon clicking busily. She wanted to continue with phase two as soon as possible.

The mirror on the dresser remained dark and still.

7

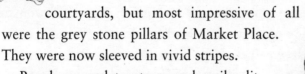

When the town of Whitby awoke and the early risers began their Sunday, they were startled to see what had appeared overnight. Throughout the East Cliff, colourful decorations now brightened the black bollards and railings. Spandrels of crocheted flowers webbed the corners of the narrow passages leading to the courtyards, but most impressive of all were the grey stone pillars of Market Place. They were now sleeved in vivid stripes.

People paused to stare, and smiles lit their faces. The woollen additions to the town were charming and delightful. Familiar walks through the

East Cliff became a treasure hunt and were filled with fresh interest.

Lil spent the first part of the morning giving Sally a bath, which the little dog greatly enjoyed. When they set off for the Wilson's shop, the Westie walked alongside her mistress with a skip in her step and her fur white and silky.

Lil was delighted to see the positive reaction to her handiwork; even the grumpiest Yorkshireman lifted his brows in amusement. She had wanted to brighten up the place, but hadn't been sure how her yarn decorations would be received. She almost laughed when she saw local residents taking photographs of themselves next to the jolly adornments, as though they were suddenly tourists in their own town, and everyone agreed how cheerful the knitting made them feel.

No one knew who was responsible and Lil wanted to keep her secret for as long as she could. Many tried to guess and whispered about that strange woman who wore those outlandish clothes. When Cherry Cerise emerged from her cottage in vintage orange Biba boots, yellow hot pants and a pink wig, she wondered why the locals were staring at her more than usual. Even odder, they were nodding and giving her conspiratorial winks.

When she saw the covered pillars, she gave a raucous yell and punched the air, rattling her plastic bangles.

'Oh, far out!' she cried. 'That is so funky. Lookin' good, Whitby, lookin' good!'

Reaching out to stroke the glorious knitting, she gave a little gasp and raised her sunglasses.

'Now ain't that interestin',' she murmured. 'I never expected that!'

The window of Whitby Gothic, like every other shop in the town, was in the process of getting a seasonal makeover in time for Easter. Instead of yellow chicks and cute bunnies, Lil's mum was dedicating the display to Eostre, the goddess of spring and fertility. A large papier-mâché hare, in full leap, spanned the entire space. Coloured eggs dangled below it and gleaming crystals were suspended above.

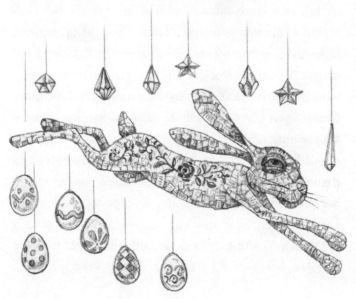

Lil pushed the door open and a tuneful jingle of hanging bells announced her.

'How does she look from outside?' her mother asked, concentrating on tying up the remaining crystals.

'Like she's pooing eggs,' Lil replied.

'Do you think I should put up the poster of Astarte as well, or would that be a bit much?'

'Umm . . . since when has that stopped you?'

'My thoughts exactly! There's a sweet figurine of her in the back. I'll prop it up in the corner.'

Cassandra Wilson extricated herself from the window and beamed at her daughter.

'Did you see what someone's done with all that knitting round the town? It's caused quite a sensation.'

Lil answered carefully. 'Yeah, it's fun,' she said, trying her best to sound casual. 'The photographer from the *Gazette* was taking pics in Market Place just now.'

'Ooh!' Mrs Wilson leaned into the window again and craned her neck round, but couldn't see that far up the street.

Lil settled Sally in a basket behind the counter and sat herself on the stool. She let her gaze wander round the shop, hoping her mother wouldn't go on about the knitting.

Whitby Gothic was crammed with everything a modern witch could wish for. There were wands of

120

every shape and size, made from quartz, metal or carved wood. The range of incense took up eight shelves and scented candles filled another five. There were pewter goblets, trinkets, talismans, pendants, dowsing pendulums, ornate candlesticks, scrying glasses, deity totems, wind chimes, clothing, books and posters. Then there were the more touristy items: the tea towels, witch dolls on broomsticks, cauldron-shaped crockery, jelly frogs and newts and plush black cat familiars.

'Have they got any idea who it was?' Mrs Wilson wondered.

Lil kept her face as straight as possible. 'Don't think so,' she said.

'You could've done that, you know.'

Lil's eyes widened a little. 'Me?'

'Yes, you're so creative and great at knitting. Maybe you should decorate the outside of the shop and get the local paper over. We could pretend we didn't know anything about it and look up, amazed, in the photos. What do you reckon? This is my "amazed" face.'

Lil relaxed as her mother practised gobsmacked expressions. She obviously didn't suspect a thing.

'I'm not going to knit stuff for the outside of the shop,' Lil said firmly. 'Besides, haven't we had enough publicity this weekend already?'

Cassandra Wilson clapped her hands with glee. 'Our website's had over a million hits!' she exclaimed.

'Your video of those skeletons has gone viral and the online business quadrupled overnight. We'll have to employ a part-timer to help if it continues.'

She gave the window another critical look.

'I'll put some of your tea cosies on show anyway,' she decided out loud. 'It'll be a great link to the mystery knitter and we might do well out of it, so you'd best rustle up some more this week. Could you do some more badges too?'

'How many hands do you think I've got? What would you like them to be of, witches knitting?'

'Oh, that would be perfect! Or toads in scarves. Or black cats in bobble hats.'

'Kittens in mittens?'

'Ooh, fabulicious! A couple of dozen if you've got time.'

'I've gone off cats. I had a horrible dream about one last night. Really freaky.'

But her mother was no longer listening. She was arranging a small display of Lil's handiwork to one side of the papier-mâché hare. The tea cosies were ingenious designs: shaped to look like funny skulls, or black with silver webs surmounted by a fluffy spider, or a Hallowe'en turnip lantern.

Watching her mother fuss with the window, adding egg cosies that looked like severed thumbs and hooked noses, Lil allowed herself a smile. Mrs Wilson never let an opportunity to push the business slip by. Making more scary-themed tea cosies for the shop would give Lil the perfect cover to create more decorations. The knitting ninja was determined to strike again as soon as she could.

Taking out her phone, she realised she hadn't heard anything from Verne. She was longing to tell him she was responsible for the big event of the day.

You OK? she texted.

It took longer than usual for him to reply.

Been a bit weird here.

There's a lot of it about. How weird?

Massive.

Been odd here too. Come over and have a look. Got something to tell you.

Too busy.

Lil frowned. Now that *was* weird. She decided to stop texting and called him instead.

'You sure you're OK?' she asked when he answered.

'No, not really.'

'Why? What's happened?'

'Something really mad. I . . . I can't talk right now.'

The call ended and Lil stared at her phone, troubled. A moment later, the bells above the shop door jingled noisily as she dashed out. She had caught an edge of fear in her friend's voice and nothing else mattered. She had to go and see him.

'Oh, Lil, hello.'

Noreen Thistlewood was usually a cheerful, well-groomed woman, but that morning when she opened the door to Lil, she seemed distracted and her hair was still damp from the shower, not its normal perfectly coiffed, heavily lacquered self.

'Is Verne in?' Lil asked. 'Is he all right?'

'Verne? Oh yes, he's in; most definitely Verne is in. No doubt about that.'

'And he's fine, yeah?'

Mrs Thistlewood didn't answer.

'You want to see him?' she asked after a pause.

Lil raised her eyebrows.

'Course you do, sorry. It's been a bit . . . odd here today. Come through and mind where you step.'

She wafted the girl inside and showed her into the living room.

Lil blinked at what she saw there. Mrs Thistlewood was compulsively house-proud and had the men in her life well trained. There was never a coffee cup out of place or a renegade sock anywhere but the laundry basket. Today however their home looked almost as bad as Lil's bedroom after the freak hurricane. The TV, DVD player and music system were strewn across the floor in various dismantled states, as were all sorts of other electrical items from the kitchen. Lil recognised parts of a food mixer, half a toaster, an egg slicer, corkscrew and many bent and twisted forks and spoons. The open carcass of a hair dryer explained Mrs Thistlewood's damp appearance.

Mr Thistlewood, Clarke and Verne were in one corner, surrounded by scattered tools and sheets of paper covered in squiggles and diagrams. Verne was still in his pyjamas and dressing gown.

'What's happened?' Lil exclaimed. 'Were you burgled?'

'*He* happened!' Clarke told her, jerking his thumb towards his younger brother.

Their father, Dennis, gave a confirming nod. 'Yep,' he said. 'Our Verne did this, made this mess, took apart just about every gadget we've got. What a tyke, eh?'

'He's a mindless vandal is what he is,' Clarke put in with a smirk.

'We don't know where to start cleaning up,' Mrs Thistlewood lamented. 'The hoover's in bits as well!'

Lil was too shocked to say anything. This was crazy. It wasn't like Verne at all. Even odder, the Thistlewoods seemed more baffled than cross. Why weren't they livid?

'I didn't do it on purpose,' Verne explained. 'I was asleep.'

'Eh?'

'Honest! I sleepwalked.'

'Get away!'

'Sounds mad, but it's true,' Dennis told her. 'I wouldn't believe it either if I hadn't seen it for myself – I came down first thing and found him, screwdriver in one hand, soldering iron in the other. I was about to yell at him when I realised his eyes were shut.'

'We didn't know what to do,' Noreen said. 'They say you're not supposed to wake sleepwalkers. So we sat and watched him finish what he was doing. Ooh, it was peculiar. I didn't like it.'

'I couldn't believe it,' Dennis continued. 'Young Klumsythumbs here was so fast and precise. There he was, eyes tight shut, bending bits of wire, soldering them, fitting them. Then, when he'd done, he lay down and had another half-hour's kip, innocent as a lamb, until Clarke woke him up yelling for his breakfast.'

'If I'd done something like this at your age, I'd have been roasted alive,' Clarke said, laughing as he playfully punched his brother on the arm.

'It's not my fault!' Verne snapped back. 'I can't remember a thing!'

'So what were you making?' Lil asked.

Verne looked embarrassed.

'Oh, show her!' Clarke said, nudging him. 'It's freakin' amazing!'

The boys and their father moved aside and there behind them was the wooden cabinet containing the old automaton.

'I've been trying to get that thing working for years,' Dennis said. 'Then, in his sleep, our Verne doesn't just fix it, he makes it do stuff it was never meant to.'

'Just show her!' Clarke cried enthusiastically. 'Come closer – you have to put the money in yourself. Trust me, it's incredible!'

Still doubtful, Lil stepped through the debris. It didn't look any different to her. Within the art-deco cabinet was the lurid diorama of an execution by electric chair. Little wooden figures surrounded the seated condemned man. They were dressed in crudely made doll-sized clothes. There was the prison warden, a priest and a guard with his hand on the big knife-switch. A woman in a black frock and hat, presumably the prisoner's wife, was perched on a bench.

Mr Thistlewood handed Lil an old penny.

'Wait a minute!' Noreen interrupted. 'You're not the nervy sort, are you, Lil? You don't have a heart condition we don't know about?'

'No,' Lil said, totally mystified.

'Go on,' Clarke urged her. 'Put the penny in.'

'No, don't,' Verne spoke up. 'It's too weird.'

'Well now I've got to!' Lil answered.

'Seriously,' Verne warned. 'Don't do it.'

His friend gave him a scowl, then pushed the coin into the slot. Verne drew back and turned away.

Lil had seen the other automata in the collection many times before and wasn't expecting much. Their

127

movements were rudimentary, driven by a single motor, with waggling heads and flipping arms. They were basic and comical and that's why she liked them.

The light in the cabinet came on and the figures commenced their routine. But there was nothing jerky or primitive about the way the priest held up his Bible, his painted wooden head moving ever so slightly as if reading from it. Standing close to the electric chair, the warden was nodding gravely, while the guard by the fatal switch seemed to be enjoying the awful moment. His shoulders moved up and down as though he was chuckling. Seated in the electric chair, the prisoner appeared to be struggling against his restraints and staring fearfully at the upside-down metal bowl suspended above his head. On the bench, his wife was sobbing and dabbing her eyes with a handkerchief.

Lil found herself caught up in the tension of this bizarre drama. Even though the performers were only dolls, they conveyed their emotions so convincingly, she almost cried out when the priest lowered the Bible and bowed his head. It was so compelling, she felt it pulling her in. Then her head began to swim.

With a sickening jolt, she found herself inside the cabinet. She was as small as the wooden figures and, to her horror, she found she had taken the place of the condemned prisoner. She was now strapped in the electric chair.

Lil cried out in shock and disbelief. This couldn't be happening, but it was absolutely real. No matter how desperately she struggled, it was impossible to get free. Above her, the copper bowl was waiting to descend, while in front the cabinet's glass window was a dark, shiny wall and she couldn't see any sign of Verne or his family beyond it.

'Help!' she yelled. 'Get me out of this! Stop it! Help!'

The mechanical drama around her continued.

The priest raised his face and Lil suddenly realised that the wooden characters resembled the people in her dreams. The priest looked like a stern Puritan, the sobbing wife was Scaur Annie and the warden was Sir Melchior Pyke. Then her eyes fell on the guard with his hand clutching the lever. His painted face was ugly and vicious, with a scar down one side, and his head was on crooked. His eyes stared straight at her and she felt the malevolence radiate from them. Then his jointed arm pulled on the switch and fiery blue sparks spat from it.

'No!' Lil pleaded.

The metal bowl came down, pressing on to her head. There was a blinding flash and she screamed.

The cabinet was filled with jagged forks of energy and the chair rocked violently. Then it went dark.

Lil fell backwards and heard Clarke laughing.

'You all right, luv?' Mrs Thistlewood asked.

Lil took several moments to catch her breath. She was back in the Thistlewoods' living room. The light inside the cabinet had gone off and the figures inside were noiselessly resetting to their start positions.

'I . . . I don't believe what just happened,' Lil uttered shakily. 'I just don't. I was there – inside it!'

'It's insane!' Clarke said. 'We can't get our heads round it either. I've had four goes and I lose it every time. You're really convinced you're sitting in Old Sparky.'

'You experienced the same thing?' Lil asked incredulously.

'Consider our minds totally fried,' Clarke said.

'But . . . how?'

Mr Thistlewood removed the wooden cover below the glass front. Lil peered inside. The space beneath the diorama was crammed with an unbelievably complex and intricate forest of levers, spindles, cams, cogs and wires.

'That still doesn't explain it,' Lil muttered.

'Don't ask me,' Verne said when he saw the stupefied, questioning look on her face. 'I haven't a clue either.'

'You honestly did this in your sleep, with your eyes shut? I've never heard of anything like it. It's not possible.'

'I know! But there it is!'

'It's creepy is what it is,' his mother said. 'It's like the thing's possessed. I won't have it in this house. It can go in the lock-up, or better still, smash it up and burn the pieces.'

'No chance!' her husband said. 'This is going in the main arcade, pride of place. We'll make a mint – more than enough to cover the mess here.'

'My mum would've rung up the telly and had every newspaper round by now,' Lil said. 'They'd go crazy for this.'

'There's no way that's going in the arcade!' Noreen said firmly. 'We'd have people keeling over with heart attacks. This is what comes of our Verne watching

131

too many horror films. No more of that, young man.'

'Truth is, Lil, we don't know what to do,' Mr Thistlewood said. 'This isn't normal science; it's probably something more in your mum and dad's line.'

'Magic?' Lil asked, almost giggling. 'There's no such thing.'

'Our Verne isn't a wizard,' Noreen agreed. 'It's just his hormones.'

'I *am* here!' Verne interrupted angrily. 'I've had enough. I'm going to get dressed.'

He stomped into the hall and Lil followed him.

'You want to come over to the shop to get away for a while?' she asked. 'I can show you this knitting . . .'

'Knitting?' the boy cried. 'Why would I want to see gormless knitting?'

'It's not gormless! It's wonderful. Come look.'

Verne rounded on her. 'Didn't you just see what I did in there, in my sleep? I created something mental. Didn't you hear my dad? It's not normal. There's got to be something seriously wrong with me! What if . . . oh, just get lost and leave me alone!'

He stormed up to his bedroom and slammed the door.

Lil felt as though Verne had slapped her. He'd never shouted at her like that before.

A comforting arm slipped round her shoulders.

'He doesn't mean it,' Mrs Thistlewood said. 'He's

had a rough night, as you can imagine. He's strung out and shocked, in every sense, by that thing in there. We all are.'

'Yes, I understand that. It's not every day you get electrocuted.'

'I wonder if what happened to you triggered something? He was so wowed by that skeleton coming through your window. He's got such an imagination that one. Perhaps I should call the doctor.'

'Tell Verne to text me when he's feeling better. I'll go back to the shop.'

'Hang on till I make myself presentable and I'll come with you, luv. Could do with a natter to your mum.'

Soon after, Verne heard the front door close and he felt ashamed for the way he had treated his best friend. It had been a bewildering morning. Reaching into the pocket of his dressing gown, he brought out the mysterious golden Nimius and stared at it intently.

'This was your fault,' he whispered. 'You made me do that to the automaton. I don't know how, but you did.'

He shuddered as he felt the object turn and click in his palm.

Alarmed, the boy threw it into a drawer and stepped away. He wanted to tell someone about it and wished he had confided in Lil. But he felt guilty for having taken it in the first place and didn't want anyone to know he'd ripped it out of a dead hand.

Inside the drawer, one of the many symbols on the surface of the Nimius began to rise.

8

L il left Mrs Thistlewood in deep discussion with her
mother at the shop and took Sally for a walk.
She carried her up the 199 steps and the Westie broke
wind all the way.

When they reached the top, Lil set her down in the
churchyard and they wove a meandering path between
the blackened and weathered leaning headstones. The
graveyard of St Mary's Church stretched far along the
cliff. Lil liked to come here to clear her head when
she was troubled and she was still shaken by her
experience within the automaton. The sea air was
sharp and clean and nature's own special magic was
soon healing her frazzled nerves.

Emergency fencing blocked off the dangerous edge
and Lil sat herself on a bench with the square and
reassuringly ancient walls of the church behind her.
She had brought her journal and began sketching the
view across the harbour.

Staring over at the arch made of whalebones that commemorated Whitby's past as a whaling port, a smile lit her face. How cool would it be to cover that in knitting? It would be a terrific challenge. Could she get away with it and not be spotted? It was so open up there, with street lamps and a main road, but if she succeeded, it would cause a real sensation.

'Yes,' she said firmly. 'I'm going to do it.'

At her feet, Sally was facing the strong breeze, head held high, enjoying the feel of it coursing through her clean fur.

'You got a real cute pooch there,' said a voice. 'Looks like a polar bear cub.'

Lil turned to see the colourful Cherry Cerise advancing towards them.

'Hey there,' the odd woman said as she knelt by the dog and reached out a hand to stroke her. 'What a beauty you are. Your fur is dazzlin'; you're like a far-out detergent commercial.'

'She's deaf,' Lil told her, not sure what else to say to this local eccentric.

Cherry laughed. 'Don't matter none,' she said. 'This adorable

136

darlin' knows I'm friendly, don't you, baby lamb?'
She stroked Sally's head and the Westie pushed
contentedly against her hand.

'She's not a puppy you know; she'll be sixteen this
year.'

'Then she's an old broad like me, still lookin'
fabulous in her twilight years.'

Sally rolled over to have her tummy tickled.

'You're honoured,' Lil remarked. 'She never lets
strangers do that. She normally bites them.'

'Her and me both, honey.'

Lil chuckled out of politeness.

Cherry removed her oversized sunglasses. Her false
eyelashes were caked in mascara, but the eyes they
framed were startlingly pale and she blinked in the
sunlight.

'Mind if I park my bony ass next to you?' she
asked. 'I'm pretty limber for my age, but them 199
steps are still murder – 'specially in a pair of kinky
boots . . . I'm pooped and my toes feel like bananas.'

Lil slid along the seat to make room, still struggling
for something to say. She wished Verne was here to
help.

'As long as you didn't count them on the way
up,' she managed, after a pause. 'If you get it wrong,
then . . .'

'Oh, sweetheart, I'm not a tourist. I know all the
myths there are about this place, probably more than

you. If you miscount the steps, you croak before the end of the year, yeah, yeah. You can't step out your door without trippin' over some legend or superstition. Bet you didn't know that under this very cliff are caves and tunnels where a secret and ancient tribe of fisherfolk used to live? And beneath that, running right below this town and under the river, is a giant sleeping serpent?'

'I've never heard that. Did you just make those up?'

'Aufwaders aren't even a mangled memory no more,' the woman said enigmatically. 'Old truths have been forgot. Land sakes, people, you threw away what was real and ran to embrace cotton-candy whimsy instead. This island's bones are cemented over and y'all were happy to let it happen. That'll cost you mighty dear.'

Lil wondered how soon she could leave without appearing rude. Verne was right: this woman was nuts.

'Whatcha writin'?'

Lil tucked the journal under her legs. 'Nothing, just doodling.'

'Spicy poetry to a secret lover, huh? I won't tell.'

'No! Nothing like that!'

'Jeepers, I used to do it all the time at your age. I had such a crush on my chemistry teacher, I learned the whole of the periodic table to impress him, then I ruined everything by blowing up the lab.'

Lil didn't know how to respond to that.

'Hey,' Cherry said, swinging her bright orange vinyl shoulder bag on to her knees and delving inside. 'You want a Whitby Lemon Bun? I got some from Botham's the bakers. Here.'

Lil declined.

'Oh, go on, I'm not a stranger. I've lived in this place twenty years. Might be a bit kooky, but I'm the most harmless gal you'll ever meet.'

'Thanks, but no.'

'Sure? It'll stave off any borborygmus.'

Lil started. '*What?*'

'Don't sweat, it's not an infectious disease. It means . . .'

'Tummy growls – I know.'

'That's right. You're pretty bright, kid.'

'My name's Lil, and that's Sally.'

'Call me Cherry.'

'OK, and go on then, I will.'

Cherry handed her a Whitby Lemon Bun and bit into another. They were a local speciality, made from sweet dough like an iced finger but with candied fruit added to the mix.

'You're eating it wrong,' Lil told her. 'You're supposed to tear off the top, turn it over and make a sandwich with the lemon icing in the middle. Only tourists eat them the normal, boring way.'

Cherry laughed and almost choked.

'Two decades and I'm still a clueless outsider!' she

cried, finishing off the first, then tackling a second the Whitby way and agreeing it was better.

'Your name's Cherry Cerise, isn't it?' Lil asked chewily. 'That's unusual.'

'Stage name, honey, but I like it better than my real one.'

'You an actress?'

'Heck, no!'

'Singer?'

'Only in the tub; sound like a constipated corncrake.'

'OK. I give up. I can't guess.'

'Nobody asked you to try.'

'American though, yes?'

'Canadian.'

'You've got a very individual, quirky fashion style.'

'Brash and loud, you mean. The seventies were my era, baby. I like to think I'm a walkin' tribute to all that – a two-legged work of art or a trashy memorial. Can't work out which.'

'You're definitely a bit of a mystery. People around here don't know much about you.'

'Like it that way. Can't stand nosy parkers. Your clothes aren't exactly run of the mill neither – unless the mill is in Transylvania. I like your badge though.'

'Thanks, I made it. I've got loads. I wear a different one every day.'

'That's neat. I like your blue fringe too, Lil. I've got a wig in peacock blue.'

'My full name is Lilith Morgana Hawthorn Blossom Minerva Tempestra Wilhelmina Wilson.'

'Oh dear Lords! You should sue!'

It was Lil's turn to laugh.

'Saw you on the TV news last night,' Cherry said, changing the subject suddenly. 'Chillin' stuff. You were one brave young lady.'

'Wasn't much else I could do. Nothing brave about it.'

'That corpse wasn't just randomly blown in by the wind, ya know. That was intentional. That skeleton sought you out. I wonder why?'

'You sound like my mum and Verne. Which reminds me, what were you doing out on the bridge that night?'

Cherry's pale eyes narrowed.

'Remindin' myself I was alive, kid,' she said.

'Verne said you were waving lights about.'

'Verne? Oh, the weedy little matchstick who went past? He almost got himself drowned. He your boyfriend? The one you're writin' kissy-kissy poetry for?'

'I'm not doing that! He's my friend, not boyfriend!'

'Whatever you say.'

Lil frowned. Cherry had evaded her question.

'Going back to that skeleton,' the woman said.

'Word is, the skull's gone AWOL.'

'Nothing to do with me. We've got more than enough ghoulish stuff in the shop.'

'That's right; you folks run the hoodoo store in Church Street, don't you? Worst thing ever happened to this town was Bram Stoker writin' that dumb Dracula book. Look what it brings to the place: hordes of bozos playing dress-up, pretendin' to be witches and vampires and Victorian dudes with ray guns.'

'My mum and dad are witches.'

'Oh, bless your heart, honey, no they're not. They're just overgrown teenagers livin' out their fantasies with cloaks and candles, and you know it.'

Lil coughed in surprise. That was a bit near the knuckle. She might think that about her parents, but it wasn't polite for this weird woman to come out and say it to her face.

'It's dangerous too,' Cherry went on. 'All those things in your store do have a certain power, but should only be handled and used by people who know what they're doin', not put on display like so many cans of soup, attractin' who knows what.'

'It's just merchandise.'

'There's too much celebration of the negative around here, all the black robes, the morbid imagery, the trappings of darkness. It gets noticed. It has an effect.'

'Noticed by who? I know the vicar doesn't like it

and thinks we worship the devil, but that's a load of rubbish. "Religious intolerance" my mum calls it.'

'Meh,' Cherry said with a dismissive shrug, gazing out to sea. 'The devil was invented by Christians. They've been fizzin' with intolerance of this 'n' that for two thousand years, what do you expect? But there are forces way, way older; three most ancient, most supreme and terrifyin' powers. You really don't want to draw *their* attention.'

'I don't believe in any of it – it's all made-up nonsense.'

'Whoa! Hold on, kid, don't disappoint. Here was me thinkin' you had brains. Magic exists. It's as real as electricity, but if my cottage needed rewirin', I'd be the biggest kind of dope to let a bunch of clumsy amateurs loose in there instead of hirin' a qualified electrician. Messin' with forces you don't understand is the deadliest thing you can do and buys you a one-way express ride to places you really don't wanna go.'

'Electricus . . .' Lil murmured absently.

'What's that?'

'Oh, er . . . nothing. And for what it's worth, my parents are white witches. They don't have anything to do with black magic.'

'Honey, only trashy newspapers and the feeble-minded see the world in black and white. There's so much more in between, and folks who don't realise that shouldn't go dabblin'. You know what really made my day earlier? All that groovy knitting down in the town. I'd like to give whoever did that a great big hug and a bunch of flowers. That's what this place needs more of: vibrancy and joy – chase all the funereal shadows away.'

Lil couldn't help tingling with pride and was determined to get the next phase done as soon as possible.

'Probably too late for that though,' Cherry continued, more to herself than Lil. 'Too much damage done already. There was anger behind that storm Friday night – a dark purpose.'

'My mum said that too.'

Cherry turned to look at her. 'Don't be offended,' she began, 'but I really do think your mom is one of the dumbest clucks I ever saw. It's like she's filled her store with kerosene and is playing with matches. She's not just invitin' trouble, she's sendin' it the cab fare and puttin' down welcome mats. Whatever's gonna happen will be part down to her. A lot of folks are gonna get burned.'

Lil rose from the bench. 'You can't talk about my mum like that!'

'Your mom and dad are irresponsible, publicity-hungry blockheads. That can't be news to you surely? They're puttin' everyone in this town at risk with that store of theirs.'

'And I think you should keep your rude opinions to

yourself, you . . . dayglo nutter! I'm going.'

Lil gave Sally a tap and the little dog followed her through the graveyard, back towards the steps.

Cherry watched them leave.

'Dumb kid's got no idea what's goin' on,' she murmured. 'There's a necklace of three ammonites round her neck and I bet she don't even know it's there. Why did Scaur Annie have to pick on her? I'm surprised the little lady's held out so long already. She should be dead by now. Another day or two will do it.'

Replacing her sunglasses, she stared out to sea once more. 'And the same for the rest of us poor saps,' she added. 'When it hits, it's gonna be savage and without mercy. None of us won't stand a chance and, to my shame, I can't think of a single thing I can do about it. This old witch is fresh outta ideas.'

Lil spent the rest of the afternoon in a temper. She was angry at what the crazy woman had said, especially as some of it rang true. She was angry at herself too; she had allowed herself to like Cherry Cerise.

Sally lay curled up on the fleecy blanket next to her and Lil's knitting needles clacked furiously. She still hadn't heard from Verne, which made everything worse. Eventually she fell asleep with her knitting on her lap.

The bare light bulb above fizzled and failed. Soon her room was in darkness. On the dresser the mirror began to ripple and the hideous skull came through the molten glass. With its lank hair snaking round it, the foul face advanced towards the sleeping girl. The jaw opened and the voice came hissing urgently.

'The Nimius grows in might! Melchior Pyke's strength is waxing. Annie must pour out her power. The East Cliff must be protected. Surrender to me; I must possess you completely. Do not fight me, child. I must have dominion. See how the villain used and tricked me.'

'Dominion . . .' Lil whispered. 'Surrender to Scaur Annie . . . pour out her power . . .'

The years unravelled and she was the seventeen-year-old ragged witch once more, walking barefoot under the moonlight through the long grasses on the cliff. Melchior Pyke was beside her. The tension between them was brittle.

'If you are to know my secret,' she said at last, 'you must swear never to speak it to another. Only the witches of this town have known the truth of it.'

'You have my solemn word as a gentleman, and as the man who loves you.'

'Then I shall surrender my secret unto you. 'Neath this cliff there be tunnels, and a hidden folk who none can see, save them what's blessed with the sight.'

'A hidden folk?'

'Aye,' she said keenly. 'Aufwaders they call

themselves and there's nowt they don't know about the sea and her moods. When my mam died of plague, it was them who came and took me in till the pestilence burned itself out in Whitby. They're my family now.'

Melchior Pyke hung his head.

'That's why I couldn't tell you!' she said. 'I couldn't give them away.'

'Aufwaders,' he repeated.

'Aye, fisherfolk. The best and biggest-hearted friends I ever knowed. You should hear their tales of olden days.'

'Faeries?' he asked. 'You're telling me you visit sea faeries? Are there Oberons and Titanias of the waves?'

'I didn't say such. You . . . you don't believe me.'

'These are but infants' fancies.'

'They are real as you and me!' she said vehemently. 'Ask your leering manservant. He's seen them often enough. They've told me as how he's spied on them. He scares them. They see the badness in him.'

'Mister Dark would think his master's wits were wandering if I asked such a question. If this is all you have to say then I will return to the inn. The hour is late and I have much to do on the morrow. This will be my final week in Whitby. My work here is almost completed.'

'My lord!' she cried, clutching his hands. 'On my life, I swear it. May the Three punish me if I speak false.'

'You talk of uncanny friends that I cannot see,' he said, with disappointment in his voice. 'When you brought me up here, I had hoped you were going to open your heart to me at last. My feelings for you are sincere and yet you still do not trust me.'

Annie watched him walk away.

'My love!' she implored. 'I speak truly!'

'Fevered fables,' he called back.

'They *do* dwell down there!' she insisted, running after him. 'Galder, Hesper and Nettie – they are dear as sisters to me.'

'And Puck, Peaseblossom, Caliban and Ariel are my brothers,' he sighed with a shake of his head. 'I have been teased enough this night.'

But Annie would not give up. 'The lord Esau is their chief elder,' she continued. 'In his chamber there is a pool where the tears of a monstrous serpent, named Morgawrus, collect.'

Melchior Pyke turned to her. 'Is there no end to this?' he asked sorrowfully. 'Must you persist? I had longed to take you to my grand house near London, but now that cannot be. You spurn the open honesty I offered and have bruised my reckless heart. When I depart Whitby, I shall voyage to a far country and never return.'

'No!' she pleaded. 'I will do anything! Do not leave me. I would never deceive my first and only love.'

'A pool of serpent's tears!' he scoffed.

'I have seen it with mine own eyes!'

'Then collect some in a bottle and bring it to me for study,' he suggested with a laugh.

Annie drew away in horror at the idea.

'I could not do that,' she murmured, aghast.

'No,' he agreed. 'Of course not. You're as like to spin a rainbow from the beards of fish.'

He had reached the top of the church steps and began striding down them, leaving her behind.

'I will do what you ask!' she called after him in a pitiful voice. 'I will fetch you proof!'

In Lil's bedroom Sally was snapping at the skull, leaping over Lil to bite the trailing hair. The hideous head rose up and hissed at the little dog, but the empty eye sockets saw something perched on the bedpost. The same tiny something that had nudged Sally to awaken her – a mouse with pale blue eyes.

The skull snarled and shook its mane of tangled hair.

Lil groaned and stirred, muttering, 'Serpent's tears . . .'

The skull retreated back to the mirror, where it sank into the rippling glass. Sally barked and fell off the bed, then barked even more, jumping up at the dresser and scrabbling at it with her paws.

Disoriented, Lil sat up.

'Sally,' she scolded. 'Hush, stop that.'

The girl picked the dog up and soothed her.

'Did you fall off the bed and frighten yourself?' she asked. 'Poor Sal.'

The Westie's barks eased, but she continued to glare at the mirror with her milky eyes.

'Silly old dog,' Lil said. 'There's nothing there.'

Her room looked the same as ever. Even the mouse had gone.

9

Across the harbour, Verne had spent the day helping his father and brother clean up the mess. At bedtime, he entered his room apprehensively.

There was a faint smell of lavender. Changing into his pyjamas, he discovered several pouches of the stuff dotted about his pillows. His mother had been taking tips from Mrs Wilson. The boy pulled a face and put them in a drawer.

The gleam of gold shone up into his eyes. That strange treasure glittered among his socks. Verne stared at it. He didn't know what it was, but it had to be responsible for his freaky sleepwalking.

'You're not going to make me do that again,' he told it. 'You're going back to the beach tomorrow. Or I might even chuck you in the river.'

He suddenly felt extremely foolish, snarling at his socks and underpants. Reaching into the drawer, he took out the Nimius.

'I'm cracking up,' he said. 'You're probably just some fancy snuffbox. Lil's always telling me there's no such thing as magic. She should know.'

The light winked and glanced off the richly decorated surface as he turned the precious object over. It really was an impressive marvel of craftsmanship and Verne was certain it was worth thousands of pounds. Then he noticed one of the symbols was raised higher than the others. He was sure it hadn't been like that earlier. Curious, he ran his fingertip over it. It was a triangle with a straight line cutting through the topmost point. Verne wondered what it meant.

Lil would know, or at least she could look it up in one of the books in the shop. While Verne was fiddling with his phone to take a photo to send her, his thumb pressed the symbol accidentally and it clicked down.

The boy felt the treasure judder and he almost dropped it. Something was happening. His eyes grew round and wide and he stared at it intently. There was a movement inside. The Nimius was trembling and shaking, as if an internal gyroscope was spinning furiously. He could feel it pulling upwards.

Verne gripped the object with both hands. He was feeling strange, almost giddy, and his heart was pounding. Next moment his head struck the ceiling and he realised he had risen off the floor. He was floating in the air.

'No way!' he gasped. 'Ow!'

Pushing against the ceiling with one hand, he held out the golden treasure with the other. At once he slid across the room and crashed against the wall. The Nimius fell from his hands and he dropped like a stone on to the bed below.

Breathless with shock and excitement, Verne grabbed it again and up he rose.

'OK,' he said cautiously. 'Let's try this . . .'

Clasping the Nimius firmly, he experimented by moving it from left to right and found he could roughly steer it. When he lowered it, his slippers bobbed across the carpet. He lifted it and was headbutting the ceiling again.

Verne started giggling. He held the Nimius out in front of him and floated forward, then he rolled it over slowly and did a somersault.

'Yes!' he cried. 'I'm flying! I *knew* there was magic – I knew it, knew it, knew it!'

His laughter was cut short as the bedroom curtains were suddenly yanked apart and the window lock unfastened itself. The window was flung wide open and Verne shot into the night like a bullet.

The lights of Whitby were gleaming in the darkness. With the salt sea air streaming into his face, the panicking boy soared over the quayside. Flying above the rooftops of the West Cliff, he clutched tight hold of the Nimius, terrified in case it pulled free of his hands and he fell to his death. Verne was no longer in control and he was mortally afraid. He tried closing his eyes, but not seeing where he was going was even worse. Magic might be real, but it was also incredibly alarming!

Swooping between chimneys and scattering their smoke, he rushed over the pantiles, startling roosting gulls. Some launched themselves at him, shrieking in his ears, but he was too swift. He whisked away over the quaintly named Khyber Pass, then over the Royal Crescent, where Bram Stoker had stayed long ago and dreamed of Dracula.

The Sunday night streets were almost deserted. The few souls who wandered did not glance up, so no one saw the young boy flying under the stars. With every wonderful moment, Verne's terror gradually faded. There was so much to see and it was glorious.

The steeple of St Hilda's Church swept into view and Verne found himself circling it three times. He flicked the weathervane with his slippered toes and sent it spinning. Then he was off again. The bare trees and lawns of Pannett Park spread below him. When he reached the museum at the centre, his progress slowed and he descended gently, bobbing just above the lead roof.

The boy felt a pang of disappointment. Was this the end of his aerial tour? He had no idea how he was supposed to get down. He clasped the Nimius tightly to his chest as he gazed around. As he rose in the air once more, he realised with a grin that he was back in control.

Verne spent the next half hour swooping round the deserted park like a giddy swallow. Keeping low to the ground, he practised every manoeuvre he could think of. When he felt confident, he raised the Nimius high and left the park behind. He had seen enough of the West Cliff. Now he wanted to zoom across the river – it was time he paid Lil a visit on the old side of town.

Returning over the rooftops, keeping the sea on his left, he couldn't resist flying under the whalebone arch. Then, floating higher, he stood on the plinth next to the statue of Captain Cook. Leaning on a bronze arm, Verne took a moment to gaze across the harbour and drink in the view.

The ragged crown of the abbey towered

majestically in the distance, rearing high over the glittering lights of the eastern shore. There was a local legend that no birds could fly over those holy ruins. Verne wondered if that rule applied to boys in pyjamas. How incredible it would be to dart up there and weave in and out of the gaping windows, maybe even land on the very top and yell out in triumph, claiming the spot as his very own.

With a cheeky salute to the captain, he headed towards the river, imagining the shock on Lil's face when he knocked on her window.

Sailing past the street lamps, Verne drew close to the quayside and was just pondering whether to dart in and out of the masts of the fishing boats, or skim the calm waters of the harbour like a dragonfly, when he felt the air around him crackle then thicken like glue. A powerful force was pushing against the Nimius. It punched into his stomach and he was sent scooting backwards.

Verne spun round. He didn't understand what had happened. He held the treasure out in front of him again and flew forward, but as soon as they reached the harbour wall, the same resistance bounced them away. Verne felt the magical device tremble in his hands, as if it was just as surprised and bewildered as he was.

Flying along the river's edge, he discovered there was no way through the mysterious invisible barrier.

Trying another tactic, Verne rose higher and higher, testing the unseen wall with his feet. The town of Whitby dwindled below, but there was still no way through to the East Cliff.

'Weird,' Verne muttered as he came drifting down again.

In his hands he felt the Nimius buzz and turn. Verne found he had lost control again as he rocketed back along the river, towards the sea. The boy saw the pale sands of the shore rushing beneath. The long stone causeway of the West Pier whizzed by and then he was flying to the lighthouse at the far end.

Spiralling up round the weathered, sandstone tower, Verne landed on the high balcony that surrounded the lantern room. Why had he been brought here?

He didn't want to wait and find out. This was a dark, lonely spot, jutting out into the North Sea. He was suddenly tired and bitterly cold. All he wanted was to return home and collapse in his warm bed.

Lifting the Nimius, he was disconcerted when nothing happened. The magical device refused to obey. Within the golden casing, an intricate mechanism was clicking and whirring softly. Verne felt another of those strange symbols pushing up from the surface.

Cautious, in case it flew off without him, he parted his fingers in time to see a small design slide aside to allow a purple and orange ametrine crystal to rise up.

The crystal had been cut and polished into an oval lens. Verne held his breath and marvelled as a beautiful glow welled up inside it. Moments later, the top of the lighthouse was ablaze with a ravishing gold and purple light. It shone over the waves, reaching down into the deep, then it flared and flashed and furled up like a fan, focusing into a slender beam that sliced through the darkness. Shining a path across the water, it passed over the sand, then up the West Cliff, over the grand hotels and beyond.

Amazed, Verne watched it dance along the buildings like a jittery searchlight, moving rapidly from house to house. The enchanted beam glittered in every window, from the North Terrace to the East, over the Khyber Pass and then down to the quayside, gleaming across his own home above the arcade and as far down Pier Road as his eyes could see.

'What are you looking for?' he murmured. But even as he spoke, he knew there was some other purpose behind this bizarre display, one he couldn't guess at. The brilliant ray swung towards the harbour wall, to shine across the river and the dwellings of the East Cliff. But it met the same invisible power that had prevented Verne flying over there earlier. The beam flickered and trembled. It burned more brightly than ever, but the impenetrable force thwarted every attempt to pierce it. The purple and golden light could not pass beyond the edge of the quay.

'Whatever that is,' Verne whispered, 'it's just as strong as you.'

The Nimius clicked, almost as if in agreement, and the light in the crystal faltered and died. The lens hinged down smoothly into the casing.

Verne blinked at the sudden darkness and colourful dots popped across his vision. When he lifted the Nimius to look at it, his slippers rose from the balcony and he sailed up into the air again.

'Time to go home,' he said.

Soon Verne was gliding through his bedroom window. Before he returned his golden treasure to the drawer, he examined it carefully, wondering what other marvels this incredible device was capable of. He searched the surface for the symbol that had given him flight, but it had blended in with the surrounding jumble of strange signs once more and was impossible to find.

Tracing his fingertips over the scrolling letters that spelled Nimius, Verne recalled that it meant 'beyond measure'. He considered the implications of that. There might be no limit to what it could do. He tried twisting it, to wind the hidden mechanism, but it wouldn't budge. Maybe it had done enough for one day.

Burying it under his socks again, he closed the drawer. A thousand thoughts and guesses were running through his mind. Here was undeniable proof that magic – proper, fantastic magic – was real. It would change the way everyone looked at the world, forever. That prospect and the grave responsibility of it all made him frown, but that misgiving vanished when he remembered the sheer joy of flying over Whitby.

Sinking back against the pillows with his hands behind his head, Verne let out an exhausted but contented sigh.

'That,' he declared, 'was the most epic night ever. What next?'

His world was charged with excitement. He couldn't believe his luck in finding the Nimius.

But then a frown returned to his face. It was Sally who had found it and Verne's guilt troubled him. It was time to confess everything to Lil. It was only right he should share this awesome discovery with her. Besides, he wanted to. Together they could decide what to do about it. He thought about sending her a text straight away, but before he could even reach for his phone, he was sound asleep.

Throughout the West Cliff, the inhabitants of Whitby

dreamed deep and long as a great enchantment began working on them.

Too angry to sleep, Tracy Evans lay on her bed, surrounded by the empty crisp packets, chocolate wrappers and biscuit crumbs that told of an evening of vexation and moping. She had been having another text argument with her boyfriend, who didn't believe her about the supernatural goings-on at the previous night's seance. The row had escalated, with cruel names called on either side, until finally he finished with her for good.

Running through the texts over and over, the injustice of being called a liar inflamed Tracy's anger and resentment. She wasn't a particularly honest person, but this time it wasn't fair. Something weird *had* happened during the seance. Bev and Angie would back her up, but she knew he wouldn't believe them either.

She fired off a few more spiteful insults, but he was no longer replying. Throwing the phone down in disgust, she switched off her bedside lamp and seethed in the gloom.

'I hate you,' she said through clenched teeth. 'I hate everyone. Hate, hate, hate!'

A chill crept over the room and the flesh on Tracy's bare arms prickled. She shivered and pulled the duvet over herself. Moments later her phone beeped and she snatched it up eagerly. But the new text wasn't from her ex-boyfriend and the name attached wasn't one she recognised.

'Dark,' she read aloud. 'What's that mean?'

Curious, she read the message.

He was not worthy of you

Tracy agreed with that and replied quickly.

Bev? That you?

My name is Dark. You reached out to me last night and I answered. Why did you run away?

Tracy sat up.

'Can't be,' she breathed in disbelief.

Is this a wind-up? Ghosts can't send texts.

This night anything is possible. Would you prefer to hear my voice? Shall I speak to you through this instrument?

Go on.

The phone rang.

'Who is this really?' she demanded.

The deep, silken voice that answered sent a delicious tingle through her.

'I have told you,' it said. 'My name is Dark.'

'And you're a spirit, using the phone? Yeah, right. Didn't know there was an app for that.'

'I am the troubled shade of a man who lived here long ago. Your pain and anger have drawn me to you, Mistress Evans. You are the light that has guided me through the cold, pathless deeps.'

Normally, Tracy would have snorted with scorn

162

at such a cheesy line, but there was something about the rich, attractive voice that made her blush with pleasure and an insidious power began to creep over her.

'So where are you now?' she asked. 'Is there a phone box in the cemetery?'

Behind her a solid black shadow rose up the wall, the tall, sinister silhouette of a man with a crooked neck. Tracy was too focused on her mobile to notice.

'I am in your hand,' the voice lied. 'Within your talking instrument.'

'You're in my phone? How?'

'Strange powers are at work tonight. Many things are now possible. Two opposing forces have seized control of this town: a witch's curse and a device called the Nimius. Go, observe your parents if you do not believe me.'

Tracy rose and left her room. Her mother and father were usually both snoring loudly at this hour, but she found them sitting on the bed in the dark, dismantling their alarm clock, radio and electric blanket.

'What's going on?' Tracy cried. 'What are you doing?'

'They cannot hear you,' Mister Dark told her. 'The Nimius controls them.'

Tracy went out on to the landing once more and looked into her brother's room.

Ten-year-old Liam was cross-legged on the floor, surrounded by pieces of a Disney night light and radio parts. Tracy watched as his fingers swiftly started pulling his games console apart.

'In every home this side of the river, the same thing is happening,' Mister Dark said. 'Preparations are being made for the coming battle. The two cliffs will go to war. There will be no survivors.'

'What?' asked Tracy groggily. A small part of her was wondering why this didn't frighten her; surely she should be panicking and trying to call someone for help? She shook her head, but she couldn't resist the lulling words of Mister Dark that were so comforting to hear. Everything felt safe when she listened to him.

'None except you, Mistress Evans,' the controlling voice continued. 'I shall save you. I have already shielded you from the influence of the Nimius, whilst those around you dance to its whims. You shall be spared the doom that approaches.'

'Me?' Tracy asked, struggling to take it all in. 'Why me?'

'Because we are alike, you and I. You feel the world is against you, a foe to be fought, and no one understands or listens. You think you are alone.'

'It's like you know me.'

'And you have a pretty neck.'

Tracy gazed at the phone in her hand and smiled. Mister Dark's words were as mesmeric as the forces that controlled her family. She was numb to the real horror of what was happening and she wandered back into her room.

'You think I'm pretty?' she asked.

'To me you are ravishing, Mistress Evans. I could eat you up.'

'Call me Tracy. Wow. You sound so nice. Could . . . could I see you? Is that possible?'

'You would like to look upon me? See my face?'

'Duh! Not fair you can see me but I can't see you.'

'Quite so. Then you may.'

165

'Hang on, you're not another of them skeletons, are you?'

'No. I promise. But to clear the veil between us you must first surrender an offering – of blood. Just three dainty drops to strengthen and seal our bond, smeared across the glass of this talking instrument. It is a small price, is it not?'

Tracy was already pulling a drawing pin from her wall and jabbing it into her thumb. Hastily, she squeezed three drops on to the phone's display and wiped them over it.

Mister Dark uttered a deep, relishing breath and beneath the scarlet streaks the phone screen went murky and dim. Then shimmering ripples of light ran through it and a figure began to form in the centre. It was the image of a young man with shoulder-length hair, dressed elegantly in black. His head was bowed and Tracy stared, transfixed, as he slowly raised his face.

She gasped. 'You're gorgeous! You could be in a boy band!'

Behind her, the misshapen shadow on the wall shook as if with laughter. The vision in the phone was as handsome as she could possibly imagine, with penetrating eyes, perfect unblemished skin and a seductive smile.

'Good evening, Mistress Tracy,' he greeted her. 'You think me fair to look upon?'

'You. Are. Awesome!'

'If we two could be together and escape the impending cataclysm, would you like that?'

'You mean you'd be alive and real?'

'I would be a living man, able to hold you in my arms and be your adoring, faithful suitor who would shower you with gifts.'

'Then duh times a hundred!'

'Is that yes? You desire it to be? At whatever price?'

'To get out of this dump and be with you? Bring it on! I don't care how.'

The face grinned back at her.

'Thank you, my love,' he said. 'May the Three grant us this blessing.'

'How soon?' she asked.

'When the battle is done, when the river runs red and both powers are spent. Then shall Dark arise and take you by the hand. Till then, say nothing and have patience.'

'Not a word.'

'There is but one small task I must ask of you.'

'What? I'll do anything.'

'I will tell you soon. Now sleep, beloved.'

'I won't be able to now!' Tracy protested. 'Don't go!'

'I must. The blood offering is already exhausted and I must fade.'

'I can give more!' she said, fumbling with the drawing pin.

Mister Dark chuckled softly. 'Not yet, gentle heart, but my spirit shall keep watch over you. The pact between us cannot be broken now.'

The screen grew dim and the handsome face vanished.

'Sleep,' his haunting voice told her.

'As if,' she said.

The shadow behind her raised its hand. The girl whimpered and sank on to the bed, unconscious.

'Credulous fool,' Mister Dark hissed.

10

'Wake up, please, Master Verne,' a strangely metallic voice was saying in Verne's ear. 'It is Monday morning and time to commence your day.'

Verne mumbled and rolled over. He opened his eyes and tried to work out what he was looking at.

'Dad?' he ventured.

'Mr Thistlewood is assisting Master Clarke with his motor scooter,' the odd voice told him.

Verne sat up. His father's steampunk butler outfit was leaning over him.

'Why are you wearing that?' the boy asked.

'I repeat,' the voice said politely, 'Mr Thistlewood is assisting Master Clarke with his motor scooter. He completed work on me one hour ago.'

Verne blinked.

'Stop mucking about, Dad,' he said, feeling cranky.

'I am called Jack Potts. What would you like for breakfast, Master Verne? It is my pleasure to serve.'

Verne stared at the costume more closely. This wasn't his father dressed up; this was a genuine, working robot.

'That's crazy!' the boy yelled. 'How? What? *How?*'

'A selection of juices and cereals is available,' Jack Potts informed him. 'Or I can provide a cooked option if you would prefer?'

'Erm, I'll make do with toast, thanks,' Verne said through a fixed grin.

The butler bowed then left the room.

Verne leaped to the sock drawer and yanked it open.

'Did *you* do this?' he growled at the Nimius. 'It's mad! What else have you done?'

Slamming the drawer shut again, he hurried from his room.

His mother was downstairs in the kitchen, watching Jack Potts clasp a slice of bread between his hands. The bellows in the chest puffed in and out, his eyes lit up and his metal palms turned red-hot, toasting the bread.

'Isn't he fantastic?' Noreen said when she saw her son. 'I'll never have to clean up after you slobs again. The only downside is you have to keep putting ten pences into his head to keep him going.'

Verne stared at his mother with wide eyes. Her face was more immaculately made up than usual and her hair was curled in an elaborate style he had never seen

before. But what really caught his eye was her bottom, which was juddering and joggling from side to side. It was wrapped in a preposterous contraption made from hot-water bottles, cling film and the motor from an old tape recorder, all plugged into the mains. It looked incredibly dangerous.

'It's to burn off those last stubborn ounces,' she explained, seeing the look on his face. 'Came to me in the middle of the night and I just had to get up and lash it together. Your father was the same. Only took him three hours to get our new butler working. I've been having the absolute best ideas for new gadgets.'

'Would you care for jam or marmalade, Master Verne?' Jack Potts enquired, slathering low-fat spread over the palm-printed toast with a forefinger that was made from a knife.

'I think I'll stick with cornflakes,' the boy said, backing away and wondering why his mother was so accepting of all this. It was insane. Robots like Jack Potts only existed in science fiction.

After breakfast, Verne put on his school uniform. It had been freshly pressed by the new butler. The creases in his trousers were so sharp Verne thought he could probably mow a field just by running through it and his shoes were as highly polished as a piece of Whitby jet jewellery.

'This is getting way too weird,' he muttered to himself as he fiddled with his tie. Passing his parents' bedroom he heard a high-pitched beeping noise and looked in to investigate. Jack Potts was folding clothes and placing them on the bed.

'I do believe we require more storage in here,' the robot told him.

Verne looked at the wardrobe, which was the source of the beeping. A dial was now fitted to the door and a circle of coloured light bulbs from the amusement arcade was arranged around it. One of the lights was blinking in time to the beeps.

'What's that?' Verne asked.

Jack Potts finished smoothing a silk blouse and turned to him.

'It is one of Mrs Thistlewood's ingenious inventions,' he announced. 'This is her omnifunctional personal grooming styliser and beautifier.'

'Mum's never done anything like this before,' Verne declared. 'She doesn't even know how to work the DVD.'

He peered at the dial. The settings were written in Noreen's handwriting and he read them dubiously as he clicked it round.

'*Casual daytime. Practical gym class. Professional businesswoman. Midweek evening out. Weekend impresser. Special occasion mega glam.* Is this why her hair is so Edward Scissorhands today?'

'I do not recommend further exploration,' the robot warned him. 'Would you permit me to straighten your tie?'

The thought of those mechanical hands at his throat made Verne shake his head hastily. Ignoring the advice, he opened the wardrobe.

Every light flashed and the wardrobe shook as Verne was pulled inside. There was the sound of whirring gears, whistles and buzzers and the boy's muffled howls could be heard out in the street.

Moments later there was a ping like an egg timer and Verne was spat out.

'Most becoming and individual,' Jack Potts complimented him.

Verne ran to the mirror and let out a yell. The device had curled and lacquered his hair, and his face had been painted with a blurred and wonky version of his mother's most glamorous make-up.

Rushing to the bathroom to scrub it off, he yelled again when he discovered his eyebrows had been threaded.

There came a polite knock at the door.

'Pardon me, Master Verne, you will be late for school.'

The boy left the bathroom, his face red and raw. He had managed to remove the make-up, but his hair still looked like a permed sheep.

Jack Potts attempted to pass him his coat. Verne snatched it from him, then hunted for his scarf.

'Where is it?' he asked.

'I have put it with the rest of the rubbish,' the robot replied. 'It looked too shabby and home-made for you to be seen wearing.'

'How dare you!' Verne cried. 'My best friend made that for me! Go get it right now!'

'It will be covered in slops. I could wash it today for you if you wish?'

'Too right I do!'

'Or I could make a new one? I am capable of producing a more professional and appealing muffler than that.'

'No, I just want that one and don't you mess about with my stuff again.'

'As you wish, Master Verne. I am earnestly repentant.'

'And I'm really going to be late for school now.'

Clarke had come in during the middle of this and he gave his brother a friendly thump on the shoulder. 'I'll give you a lift on the Vespa!' he offered. 'Dad and me have been tuning her up and I'm just about to give her a trial spin.'

Verne grabbed his rucksack and followed his brother outside.

Jack Potts wandered through to the kitchen, fished the scarf from the bin using a large pasta fork and carried it at arm's length on to the balcony where he set fire to it and watched it burn.

The West Cliff was busy as usual on a Monday morning. The sun was out, the gulls were making their customary racket and people were preparing to commence another working week. Verne didn't notice the strangeness at first, but as he gazed around he began to realise a change had come over this once familiar and reassuringly normal place.

A window cleaner first drew his attention to it.

The man was halfway up a ladder, whistling briskly, but his arms were folded and the windows were being cleaned by a crawling contraption made from a food mixer with chamois leather attachments dragging squeegees.

Further down the road, Verne saw a woman in her dressing gown proudly overseeing a small spinning device, wielding several dish mops and a sponge, that was busily washing her doorstep. A little way along, a man was riding a bicycle with super-suction tyres up the wall, leisurely whitewashing the brickwork.

Verne's unease mounted. It wasn't a normal Monday at all. What was going on?

The gulls overhead began to shriek more raucously than ever. A stuffed Dracula toy, strapped to a flying drone made from an electric fan, flew across the rooftops to squirt water at them.

Verne watched it pursue the gulls round the chimneys until a dinner bell began clanging and he peered down the pavement to witness an old lady setting forth in a petrol-driven supermarket trolley. She was grinning with delight and perfectly comfortable for it was decked out with lots of cushions and a tartan blanket covered her knees. It was steering itself and she was leafing through a magazine, only breaking off to ring the bell at anyone who got in her way.

'Madder and madder,' Verne murmured.

The inventions were so ludicrous it should have

been funny, but he felt only dread and a rising sense of panic.

The noise of a vacuum cleaner made him turn round. An embarrassed-looking dog was being taken for a walk by an adapted Hoover, which was poised and ready with its nozzle for the inevitable clean-up duty.

'Everyone's gone crazy,' he said to his brother. 'Just look at them. They're behaving as if it's all perfectly ordinary.'

'What you on about?' Clarke asked, following his gaze. 'It all looks fine to me.'

Before Verne could answer, an unmanned vehicle made from the chassis of an old pram, carrying the morning's post, came trundling down the road. Sets of rotating, snapping barbecue tongs were mounted on the sides and they snatched up the mail, flinging it into letter boxes.

Verne ducked as the automatic postie rolled by and two envelopes went skimming over his head, shooting with implausible accuracy through the arcade door.

'That's what I'm talking about!' he spluttered to his brother. 'That's just absurd. It's ridiculous.'

Clarke shrugged.

'Seems OK to me,' he said. 'Someone should've invented that ages ago.'

Verne stared at him in confusion.

'You can't see it, can you?' he said. 'You're caught up in it too.'

'Ha!' Clarke laughed. 'Have you been wearing lipstick?'

But Verne didn't hear him. Fear was clenching his stomach. He had the awful suspicion that somehow he was responsible for this. He felt sure the strange light that had shone from the Nimius had brought about this transformation. But how? And why? What was the point of turning half the town into crazy inventors, making the most stupid machines he'd ever seen?

'There's got to be a reason,' he told himself. 'This has to be just the start of whatever it is.'

'You going to school or what?' Clarke asked. 'Oi! Verne! Snap out of it!'

Verne started.

'Yes,' he said. 'Where's the Vespa?'

'Round the corner here,' his brother said. 'She's better than ever.'

Verne didn't know much about bikes. When he saw Clarke's pride and joy, he thought it seemed a bit bulkier than usual under the seat, and two new chrome exhausts had been added.

'I thought Dad was out here with you?'

'He's gone to the lock-up to start building the big stuff,' Clarke said. 'Now, put this helmet on, get behind me – then hold on for dear life.'

'Dear life?'

'You betcha!' Clarke whooped.

A torrent of flame punched from the exhausts. The

scooter reared up, then roared down Pier Road. Verne wailed and clung to his brother desperately as the world shot by. But instead of turning up the Khyber Pass and heading to the school, Clarke rode on to the stone pier and within seconds they were speeding over the wooden extension, scorching the planks as they went.

'What are you doing?' Verne yelled. 'We're going to crash!'

'You haven't seen what this baby can really do yet! Hold tight!'

Verne saw the end of the narrow pier come flying to meet them. He clamped his eyes shut, waiting to smash into the railing. Instead, he felt the scooter tilt back and launch. They soared through the air in a perfect arc, then plunged down towards the open sea.

Inwardly yelling, Verne held his breath.

There was a terrific splash, followed by a throaty revving, and then the Vespa was riding the waves like a jet ski. It bumped and sped over the water, sending up a spout of white foam in its wake. Clarke steered it around and they whooshed between the two piers, re-entering Whitby via the harbour. Their furious passing caused all the fishing boats to rock and Verne couldn't stop himself laughing. It was exhilarating. They charged beneath the swing bridge and tore up the river. Then Clarke drove up a slipway, left the water behind and they were back on the road again.

'Yes!' he whooped. 'The first amphibious Vespa!'

He delivered Verne to the school gates, wet but exactly on time.

'Just you wait till I fit the rocket launchers!'

'The what?' Verne cried, but Clarke was already zooming down the road.

Verne frowned and decided he really needed to speak to Lil. But that would have to wait until break.

And so the strangest school day he had ever known began.

Verne quickly noticed that most of the children who lived on the West Cliff had brought in yet more home-made gizmos. Many were simple, like automatic spectacle wipers and little gadgets that marched pens from pencil cases and waited to be told what to write, in beautiful copperplate. Others were more exotic – one girl in his class had created an 'Inkbug', a metal creature that looked like a beetle. Carrying three coloured felt tips, it crawled up and down her arm, drawing elaborate faux tattoos.

Most were mischievous. One of the boys set a clockwork 'Shoelace Muddler' on the floor, which scurried under the desks to snip through laces, tie two pairs together or tangle them irrevocably with countless knots. Another boy had invented a 'Mugly' torch that projected big noses, warts, beards and acne on to any face. He spent the first ten minutes of the lesson making a girl from the East Cliff look like a gross troll while the teacher's back was turned.

It quickly dawned on Verne that the victims of these practical jokes all lived on the other side of the river. None of *them* had brought in any strange contraptions. He stared at them curiously. The Easties were unusually quiet and solemn-looking. He noticed that the girls were wearing as much black as the uniform allowed and had painted their nails to match. They had pendants round their necks or small velvet pouches like the herb talismans sold in the Wilsons' shop. Even the boys from the East Cliff looked grave, with pale faces, and he was astonished to see that three were wearing eyeliner and one had dyed his hair.

'Gadgets versus goths,' Verne muttered under his breath, then added, with annoyance, 'and quite right too . . . destroy the stinking witches.'

He shook himself. Why had he said that?

Before he could ponder any further, Mrs Fullerton sensed something was going on and caught sight of the Mugly torch. It was confiscated straight away and then the teacher came striding towards Verne.

'This isn't a sculpture class!' she told him sternly.

Verne didn't understand what she meant until he gazed down at his desk. He jumped back so sharply his chair squealed over the floor. An aggressive-looking stick figure made from pencils, with pieces of eraser for feet, a protractor shield and a compass spear, was crouched on his desk. Next to it, in many disassembled pieces, was his pocket calculator and some of the electronics had been incorporated into the unpleasant-looking warrior.

'I didn't know I was doing that!' the boy blurted out truthfully.

Mrs Fullerton reached forward to take the figure away. As her hand came near, the compass struck out and stabbed her. She yelped in pain.

'Sorry, Miss!' Verne cried. 'That wasn't me!'

'Put it in the bin!' she demanded. 'What's got into all of you today?'

The children stared at her dumbly. Then one of the boys from the East Cliff said, in a disconcerting monotone, 'You don't live in Whitby, do you, Miss? You should go home. You don't belong here.'

'East and West only, Miss,' another told her.

'No outsiders.'

At break time, Mrs Fullerton described the experience to her colleagues in the staffroom. Some of the other teachers were just as concerned as she was, but the members of staff who lived in Whitby told them they were overreacting. Mr Derby, the Head, assured everyone there was no need to be alarmed. Mr Derby also lived in Whitby.

In the playground, the children were unusually quiet, but there was a simmering tension. No one was playing. The two groups did not mingle and there were many huddled gangs conspiring in whispers.

Verne spent most of the break trying to find Lil.

With only minutes left, he discovered her sitting in a corner, knitting quietly, surrounded by balls of wool.

'Hey!' he said. 'Been looking for you everywhere. You OK?'

'Course,' she replied. 'Why wouldn't I be?'

'Sorry about yesterday and how I treated you. I was freaked out, but that's no excuse.'

'Don't matter,' she said.

'So how's it gone with you this morning? It's crazy, isn't it?'

'What is?'

'The way everyone's acting today, and all these preposterous inventions that shouldn't work but do.'

'Don't know what you mean.'

Her disinterest began to annoy him.

'If you'd look up from your stupid knitting for a minute, you might see what's going on around you!' he said. He gave one of the woollen balls a kick, but instead of sending it rolling, he felt a crackling pain shoot up his toes and sizzle along his leg.

'Ow!' he cried, hopping in a circle. 'What was that?'

'Looks like cramp – and my knitting isn't stupid. It's wonderful. If you hadn't been so obnoxious yesterday, you'd have seen why. Your loss.'

'Well, I've got a better secret,' he snapped back. 'An amazing one! I was going to share it with you, but tough. You're as bad as the other Easties. Just another miserable goth. No, you're worse. You're just like *her* – a dirty Whitby witch.'

'Who's "her"?'

'You know! You've got the same look in your eyes.'

The bell rang, putting an end to the argument. But as the day wore on, things grew steadily worse. The gadgets became more dangerous and threatening. One was fitted with the blades of pencil sharpeners and scurried up a girl's back, shaving a stubbly path through her hair.

The children of the West Cliff laughed and so did the teacher. The girl and the others from the East side glared at them coldly.

During the afternoon break, the boy who had invented the 'Gothscalper' was cornered by his victim. She and a cluster of her friends surrounded him, chanting and pacing round and around with hands clasped. When they eventually moved away, the boy was huddled on the ground, covered in boils and howling in agony.

Then everything changed. A chill wind blew across the playground and the air became heavy and oppressive. The atmosphere was charged with aggression and hundreds of fights broke out. The possessed pupils lashed out at one another in a violent riot.

The unaffected teachers were horrified. There was nothing they could do to stop it. Eventually, someone called the police. Two cars arrived, but the officers were from both sides of the town and they joined in. School was dismissed and the fierce brawling surged out into the streets.

Verne didn't take part in the fighting; he had watched it at a distance, like a general overseeing his troops in battle. He didn't seek out Lil again. Just the thought of her made him angry and he wanted to hit her. He couldn't understand how they had ever been friends and decided she must have tricked him. That was typical of witches; they were such deceitful creatures.

He thought of the Nimius and wished he had brought it with him. It would have made short work of these ignorant heathens and he couldn't wait to be reunited with it. The mysteries of its function were clear now. The last traces of the boy's resistance had been vanquished, burned along with his scarf and a will far more powerful than Verne's own had gradually asserted itself throughout the day. He remembered the amazing things the Nimius was capable of and knew how to operate it.

After school he took the longer way home to avoid bumping into Lil. As he entered the flat above the arcade, he was greeted by Jack Potts who bowed before him.

'Welcome back, Master Verne,' the robot said. 'I have prepared for you a nutritious tea and laid out all the tools and apparatus you will require later.'

Verne looked at the butler anew. He was no longer afraid of him; a formidable intelligence now burned behind Verne's eyes.

'Call me by my true name,' he commanded. 'You know full well who I am.'

Jack Potts bowed even lower.

'I do indeed, your lordship,' he said. 'It has taken longer than I expected for you to assume total control of the child.'

'His obstinate, juvenile mind was unusually strong. But the struggle is over.'

'Congratulations, your lordship. And it is my honour to give you this. I found it whilst tidying his sock drawer.'

Jack Potts raised his metal hands. He was holding the Nimius. The boy took it reverently.

'My crowning achievement,' he said, caressing the golden treasure. 'We shall never be parted again.'

'What are your orders, your lordship? When do the hostilities commence? There are still refinements to be made, weapons to be perfected. Everyone has been most industrious throughout the day, but we are not quite ready.'

'Let it be known,' the boy told him, 'that the war begins at dawn and Sir Melchior Pyke will lead the West Cliff into battle.'

11

Tracy Evans did not attend school that day. When she awoke there had been a lengthy text waiting. Her new boyfriend gave very specific instructions, which she was to obey to the letter if she wanted to be with him.

And so she made her way down to the Scaur beneath the cliffs, picking a slippery path between the rock pools until she reached the designated spot, and there she waited. Hours passed and Tracy stood, shivering and shuffling her feet. The air that gusted in off the sea cut through her. She checked her phone constantly, but no more texts beeped in. She wished she could talk to Angie or Bev about what had happened, but Dark had sworn her to secrecy. She didn't know that her two cronies were kicking and thumping each other in the school playground because they lived on opposite sides of the town.

Eventually, the tide turned and started creeping

closer; the outlying pools and sloping black rocks were lost under the encroaching waves. Tracy began to fear she would be cut off. If she didn't head back soon, she wouldn't be able to reach the town at all.

Anxiously, she gripped her phone and sent urgent texts to Dark. There was no reply. Taking a badge from her pocket, she pricked her thumb with the pin and squeezed blood over the screen.

'Please,' she begged, with one eye on the advancing waves. 'Where are you? No one's here. You said there'd be someone here.'

Even as she snivelled, she caught sight of a round object bobbing and rolling in through the waves. It was made of metal and a little larger than a football. As it came closer, she stared in surprise, recognising it as the helmet of a Roman gladiator. The metal was rusted and fused together, but the visor grill, crest and neck guard were still identifiable.

The helmet rolled on to the rocks close by and Tracy took a step towards it. She wondered if it was worth any money and was just reaching down to touch it when the helmet flinched and took several scuttling steps backwards. Tracy gave a yell.

The helmet turned around so the visor was facing Tracy, who saw that the barnacle-covered legs of a crustacean were lifting it off the ground. Glistening black eyes on stalks poked through the grill and regarded her keenly. Then there came a burbling,

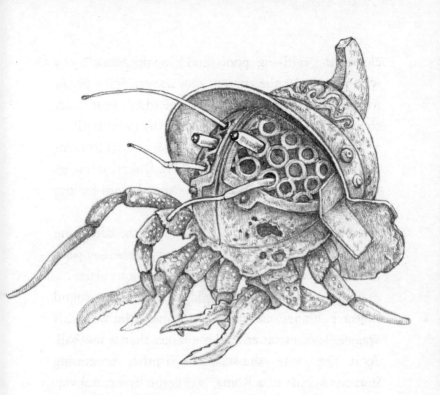

sloppy sort of sound and the creature inside spoke.

'Give,' it demanded. 'Give.'

Tracy was too taken aback to respond.

The helmet jerked forward and a hooked, crab-like pincer shot out and nipped her ankle.

Tracy yelped, then remembered her instructions. Reaching inside her rucksack, she took out her lunch box.

'Are you the emissary?' she asked. 'Sent by *Them*? Yes, of course you are. I'm to pay you with food, live food. You like the warm blood of the land, don't you?'

'Blood is the bridge! Blood is the price!' the creature said. 'Give!'

Tracy peeled back the perforated lid.

'Bit late for breakfast,' she said with a weak laugh, 'but here's Eggs and Bacon.'

Her brother's hamsters were already scrambling to get out of the Tupperware box. Tracy scooped them up briskly and handed them over.

Two pincers flashed out from the rusted helmet, seized the small animals and snatched them inside. There was a repulsive chattering of mouthparts, a slobbering and crunching of small bones.

Tracy looked on impassively, too deeply under Mister Dark's control to comprehend what she had done. The entire population of Whitby, her family, friends, everyone she knew, was going to die, but she didn't care. The only thing that mattered was being with her dream boyfriend; she had no thoughts or emotions beyond that.

When the meal was over and small, satisfied grunts issued from the helmet, she asked, 'So what's the answer?'

The eyes poked out at her again. Then they angled right and left and the helmet revolved to make sure no one else was around.

'The assurance is given,' the strange voice uttered. 'The one named Dark will be granted extra powers and, when the violence is unleashed, no hurt shall come to those who stand within the seal. That has been promised.'

'He'll be able to come through, be alive, with me, yeah?'

The eyes retracted into the shadowy interior and the helmet lifted on six segmented legs.

'With you? Yes. With you, yes. You are needed. He cannot live again without you. He values your sweet, precious life most highly.'

A scratchy sound, like cruel, thin laughter, followed. Then a wave came splashing up the rocks. The helmet jumped, almost in fear, and danced around in agitation.

'We did not speak,' it told the girl hastily. 'There are watchers everywhere. I do not know you. I must return.'

Spinning about, it set off towards the sea, charging into the water, muttering and making contented sucking noises.

'Eggs and Bacon, Eggs and Bacon,' it said with relish before being engulfed by a foaming wave that swept it away.

Tracy checked her phone and sent a text.

I did it. They agreed. Can't wait 2 c u 4 real!!!

There was no reply, but the sea came swirling around her shoes. The girl shrieked and went charging back along the submerged rocks towards the town.

*

Wandering home through the East Cliff, Lil was so preoccupied that she hardly noticed how much it had changed during the day. The cobbled streets reeked of incense and occult symbols had been painted on windows and walls. Candles flickered on every sill and there were talismans and charms nailed to every door. The only places free of this were those areas she had decorated with her knitting.

When she passed Whitby Gothic, she saw a large sign in the window that read:

SOLD OUT!
Of everything!
Closed until further notice.

Lil hurried home. The East Cliff was silent. There were no sounds of any cars and no music or TVs blared out. All she could hear was indistinct chanting.

'The till never stopped ringing,' Mrs Wilson explained when she arrived home. 'It was a feeding frenzy! And, the bizarre thing is, all the customers were from this side of town. No one from the other side even came near. The day trippers couldn't get a look in.'

'We need to order fresh stock,' added her husband.

'I should get busy with my wool then,' said Lil.

And so she spent the evening in her room with her yarn and needles, but she wasn't making things for the shop.

Sally nuzzled next to her, licking her hand whenever it was within reach. By one o'clock in the morning, Lil was ready. Her parents had gone to bed earlier than usual and she figured it was safe to creep out. It was time for the phantom knitter to strike again. Whitby's whalebone arch was about to get a colourful makeover.

Wrapping a black cloak round her shoulders, she left Sally sleeping soundly on her bed and made her way down the stairs, closing the safety gate behind her. This time she was going to need a stepladder, so she took one with her.

The East Cliff was in darkness. All the street lights had gone out and Lil wondered if there had been a power cut. Carrying the awkward ladder and a large bag, she crossed the bridge to the other side. The West Cliff was a complete contrast: every street lamp was lit and it seemed even brighter than usual. Here and there, flaring in gardens and yards, she saw stuttering blue flashes as if from welding torches, although she couldn't think why anyone would be using them at this hour. She began to wonder if tonight was really the best time for phase two of her plan. But she saw no one as she wandered up through the Khyber Pass, towards the corner of the cliff where Cook's statue and the arch stood.

With her heart in her mouth, Lil set up the ladder beneath one of the whalebones and took a long length of stripy knitting from her bag.

'Here we go,' she said.

By half past two, she'd sewn both sleeves in place on the archway and she scrambled down the ladder to admire her handiwork.

The whalebones looked fantastic; resplendent and jolly in a bright woollen rainbow. A delighted chuckle escaped her lips as she anticipated the commotion it would cause in the morning. Now for a speedy getaway . . .

'That'll make plenty of eyes pop out, kid,' a voice behind her said.

Lil jumped and spun round as Cherry Cerise came sauntering from the shadows.

'What are you doing out here at this time of night?' Lil asked.

'Shouldn't that be my line?' the woman replied, peering over her sunglasses. ''Cept I've been watchin' you so I know already.'

'You been spying on me?'

'Darn right I have. I love what you've been tryin' to do for the town, I really do. But it's too little too late.'

'Too late for what?'

'Do you really have no idea what's goin' on right now? No clue at all?'

'How'd you mean?'

The woman glanced around cautiously. 'You got problems, honey. I am talkin' huge. We need to talk. But not here. It ain't safe. Come back to my cottage.'

'Er . . . no!' Lil refused, taking up the stepladder and walking away.

'It's on the way back to your place anyways,' Cherry urged, catching up with her. 'Just five minutes. There's stuff you gotta know.'

'It's gone half two in the morning. I'm going straight home.'

'Straight home . . . through the old part of town which has turned into a badly dressed horror flick. Or didn't you notice Hallowe'en has arrived mega early to the East Cliff? And this side has turned into a cockamamie sci-fi convention via thaumaturgy. And you think everything's hunky-dory and you're just happily tootlin' on with your yarn thing. Land sakes – wise up, kid!'

Lil halted and chewed her lip as she gazed around them, taking in all the oddities. It was like she was seeing Whitby for the first time. Cherry was right; there was something really strange going on. Why hadn't she paid more attention to it?

Intrigued, she said, 'OK, five minutes.'

'Believe me, kid, they'll be the most important five minutes of your life.'

And so they walked over the bridge, then through the darkened streets of the East Cliff. Behind them the colourfully sleeved whalebone arch reared high and graceful over the town.

Stepping out from behind a parked car, Tracy Evans stared at the woollen decorations with contempt.

'Tat!' she said with a sneer.

Drawing closer, she reached up to tear them down.

'Do not touch the arch,' a voice told her.

Tracy's face lit up and she hurriedly fished out her phone.

'That you?' she asked, staring intently at the blank screen. 'I can't see you. Does it need blood again?'

'Not yet,' Mister Dark said. 'But soon, soon there will be blood, rivers of blood. At first light, this town shall be swept away and all will die. The only protection is to stand within the seal of the Lords of the Deep and Dark. Look closely at this device. I will show you the triangle, the circle and the square. You must copy them exactly, without mistake. Draw them upon the ground around you and I will dictate the words of power to inscribe within.'

'When it's all done,' Tracy said, breathless with excitement. 'When it's all washed away and gone, we'll be together, yeah? You and me? Just us two, forever?'

Mister Dark laughed softly.

'When the cataclysm destroys the town and only you remain alive, yes, I shall appear before you, within the seal.'

'And you will have new life,' Tracy said, elated.

'Yes, new, sweet life will be mine to enjoy and be refreshed by.'

'Then show me what to draw,' the girl urged. 'I'll do it perfect, no mistakes. I can't wait!'

'What a delicious darling you are,' said Mister Dark. 'But you must be swift, for I have an appointment elsewhere this night and it is an encounter I must not miss.'

'This is it,' Cherry said when they came to the entrance to one of the yards leading off Church Street. Moments later she was opening a brightly painted yellow door.

'Leave your steps out here; they're not gonna run away – unless someone from the West Cliff has been fiddlin' with them.'

Lil leaned the ladder against the wall and looked curiously at the cottage. It seemed no different from the others in the yard, except it was more cheerful. A profusion of plastic flowers was crammed into two hanging baskets and the window boxes were festooned with even more. There were crystals dangling in the windows and pouting red lips were painted round the letter box, above which a stone with a hole worn into it was suspended by a violet ribbon. Lil recognised it as a hagstone, a traditional charm to ward off witches. Cherry took it down and invited her in.

The girl stepped inside.

'Oh!' she exclaimed.

Cherry had snapped on the lights and Lil experienced a sudden explosion of pink. The walls were pink, the ceiling was pink, the woodwork, even the carpets – all vibrant shades of pink.

'Bit much?' Cherry asked. 'Pink is my go-to colour. It kinda gets carried away with itself.'

Lil took several deep breaths.

'It even smells pink in here!' she said in astonishment. 'I mean proper pink: candyfloss, blossom, Verne's mum's nail varnish, strawberry milkshakes, cupcakes, roses, bubblegum, marshmallows, Turkish delight, babies . . . that's just mad!'

'Yeah, I can tone it down if you want. Lavender any better? I never liked mauve; sounds too much like Mavis and I ain't no Mavis.'

Lil blinked. The colour was changing, softening, turning cooler as paler hues rose up from the skirting board and mingled across the walls until every trace of pink had been muted. The inside of the cottage was now the mildest milky purple and the air was rich with the scent of lavender fields at dusk.

'What's going on?' she asked. 'How did you do that?'

Cherry waved at a chaise longue covered in a flowery throw. 'You might wanna sit down before I tell you,' she suggested.

Lil frowned but did so and glanced about the cosy room. It was like nothing she'd ever seen before. The TV was moulded white plastic, shaped like a space helmet. Next to that was a smoked-glass coffee table bearing a bowl of artificial fruit and an orange Trimphone.

An old-fashioned stereogram dominated one wall and on the mantelpiece, beneath a painting of a green-faced Chinese woman, two lava lamps were glowing and glooping.

Cherry eased herself into a large wicker chair shaped like half of an egg suspended from the ceiling and stared at Lil through her sunglasses.

'Do you know who owned this place before I moved in?' she asked.

'That was way before I was born.'

'Your mom never mention it?'

'Why would she?'

'Cos the old broad in question

would've been right up her street. She was a witch – a real one. And this town has everything to thank her for. She saved it from obliteration a bunch of times.'

'Is that seriously what you brought me here to tell me?'

'I ain't crazy, kid, but I am losin' my patience. You need to realise that witches exist. I'm not talkin' about people like your folks, who enjoy dressin' up and gettin' down with nature, but people with special gifts, special powers, special responsibilities. They can see and do things that other folks can't. The old dame who lived here before me wasn't the first genuine witch to live in Whitby. This funny little town always has to have one in residence; it's a law that goes back thousands of years. This place needs protectin', guardin'.'

It was obvious from Lil's face that she didn't believe a word. 'Are you drunk or something?'

Cherry carried on. 'The very day that old lady died, her successor turned up, out of the blue. She didn't even realise why at the time, just thought she'd run out of dough and had been dumped in the back end of beyond by her louse of a manager. But she figured it out eventually. It was all part of the great plan.' She leaned forward. 'Brace yourself, you're not gonna like it, but that dumbo was me. I'm a witch.'

Lil rose. 'I'm going,' she said. 'You've had your five minutes.'

'You better start believin' honey and ditch the

denial, cos the lives of everyone you care about are at stake. This town is in danger again and this witch ain't strong enough to fight it on her own.'

'Goodnight,' Lil said with stern finality as she made for the door.

'Wait, wait!' Cherry begged. 'Haven't I already proved it by changin' the colour in here?'

'Clever lighting and air-fresheners,' Lil insisted. 'My mum and dad are always rigging the shop with cheap tricks like that.'

'Sheesh, you're a tough crowd.'

'Why don't you just get a broomstick and fly over the abbey?' Lil asked sarcastically. 'Mum'll let you have one at a discount when she gets her new stock in, if you tell the papers where you bought it. I'll believe you then.'

'I can't fly. Not many witches can. We all have different talents, different ways of focusing our powers.'

'You're a bit rubbish then,' Lil said as she pulled the door open.

'Are you so scared I can prove you wrong?' Cherry challenged her. 'Worried there really is magic in the world after all? Don't want your blinkered view turned upside down? That it? Can't deal with the truth? You really that feeble?'

Lil closed the door again and faced her.

'Go on then,' she demanded. 'Show me.'

Cherry grinned. 'That's better,' she said. 'Now, have you got somethin' colourful on you?'

'I've been sneaking about in the dark,' the girl reminded her. 'You don't wear neon for that.'

'Nothin' in your pockets?'

'What sort of a witch are you supposed to be, for heaven's sake?'

'I'm a colour witch. My power works through wavelengths and frequencies of light. The stronger the colour, the more energy I can channel. That ain't easy in this town. Colours are a primal force of nature, kid. How many times have you heard someone say they're "feelin' blue", or "green with envy", "seein' red" or "in the pink"? They don't realise it, but they're tappin' into one of the most ancient forms of magic.'

'That's the daftest thing I ever heard,' Lil said flatly.

She had been rummaging through her pockets and pulled out the bundles of red and yellow wool she had used to stitch the sleeves on to the whalebone arch.

'That the best you got?' Cherry asked. 'Guess it'll have to do.'

'Wait,' Lil muttered. Reaching further down, her fingers closed on two small objects she had forgotten were there – the fragments of her Lucky Duck. She hadn't had the heart to throw them away.

'Now you're talkin'!' Cherry cried when she saw the pieces of aquamarine glass on the girl's palm. 'Put your other hand on top and clasp them tight together.'

Feeling foolish, Lil obeyed.

Cherry took a deep breath and drew herself up. She removed the sunglasses and Lil was startled to see how fiercely those pale blue eyes were shining. Cherry raised her arms. The colour of the walls seemed to reflect off her hands, shining brighter and brighter.

Lil flinched. She felt a wriggling twitch between her closed palms. A blue light welled through her fingers and a tingling heat radiated out. Then the brilliant glow faded – from her hands, from Cherry, from the walls, from the carpet. A mellow orange flowed down from the ceiling to replace it and the air smelled of peaches and warm honey.

Only Cherry's eyes still blazed blue and she stared fixedly ahead as though blind.

'Take a look, kid,' she said.

Lil's hands were trembling. Cautiously she peered inside.

The Lucky Duck was whole again – and it was moving. It was alive! It swam about the pond of Lil's palm, the cartoon-like eyes blinking while the tiny beak opened and closed. Then it gazed up at the girl, winked and gave a high-pitched quack.

Lil cried out and almost dropped it. Cherry laughed

and her eyes became pale once more. The Lucky
Duck's movements ceased and it was just an ornament
again.

'How's that for clever lightin'?' she said, putting
her sunglasses back on.

Lil stared at the inert duck, speechless and
dumbfounded. After several, incredulous moments,
she murmured, 'Can I have a cup of tea? I think I need
to sit down.'

'I know, kid,' Cherry said sympathetically. 'And
I wish I could say you'll get used to it, but you never
do. And you'll be seein' a lot more unbelievable stuff
real soon. Fact is, you've been seein' plenty already,
but you've been too pig-headed to let yourself admit
it. Ain't easy when the world you think you know is
blown apart. I'm sorry you got snarled up in all of it.'

Still struggling to comprehend, Lil returned to
the chaise longue. The walls were slipping from
orange back to pink. She gazed at them blankly. The
one solid, unshakable foundation of her entire life
– that there was no such thing as magic – had been
demolished.

'Is it any wonder I never usually let anyone in
here?' Cherry said, nodding at the fluctuating hues.
'Every house has an atmosphere and the folks who
live in it charge it like a battery with their own unique
energies. In a witch's home, those vibes are way more
powerful. Me being a colour witch, well, it's like

livin' inside one of those mood rings. Suits me fine, but other folks would freak. Mind you, when I'm in a brown funk, even I have to get outta here!'

Lil was too shocked to answer. The whole experience was so weird, she felt dazed and light-headed.

'I'll get you that tea,' Cherry said kindly. 'Best magic potion there is.'

She disappeared into her kitchen, chattering lightly the whole time.

'So what made you start the knitting thing in the first place?' she asked. 'Whatever it was I approve wholeheartedly and there's somethin' about it you really oughta know . . .'

'I'm going to sabotage the Goth Weekend,' Lil said. 'These were just trial runs.'

Cherry returned, bearing two mugs of green tea. 'Supposed to boost the brain,' she said. 'And right now we need to be extra smart. Sabotage how?'

Lil clasped the mug under her chin. The fragrant steam started to revive her.

'I was going to knit grave cosies,' she said.

'What the heck are they?'

'Same as tea cosies, but bigger – for headstones. Bright grave cosies to put over as many headstones in the graveyard as I could.'

Cherry spat out a mouthful of tea as she honked with laughter. 'Oh, I love it!' she cried. 'All those pretend vampires and zombies gaggin' to have moody photos taken in the gloomy churchyard. Imagine the annoyance on their grey faces!'

'I reckon I could get about fifteen or twenty cosies done by then,' Lil said.

'I wish you'd thought of it sooner. Cos, you know, there won't be any Goth Weekend this year.'

'I hadn't heard it's been cancelled.'

Cherry's face grew serious. 'Honey, *Whitby* has been cancelled. This little town simply won't *be* here in a few weeks' time. It'll be drowned beneath the sea and the rest of us with it if we don't clear out.'

'*What?*'

'You got some serious heavy-duty blinkers.'

Lil sank back in the seat as she began to piece together the strange occurrences of the past few days.

'The name Scaur Annie clangin' any bells?' Cherry asked.

The girl's eyebrows lifted. 'That name . . . I've been having dreams,' she said. 'Really vivid ones. In the dreams, I'm her, Scaur Annie.'

'They weren't dreams, honey. Scaur Annie was a real person who lived here hundreds of years ago. The story of the ragged witch and the gentleman was well known locally at one time. You never come across it before?'

'Never. What happened to her?'

'The story goes she was a young, and obviously

dumb as a brick, witch who fell in love with a visiting bigwig, Sir Melchior Pyke, a genius mad scientist and more besides.'

'He was a cruel user!' Lil interrupted sharply. Then she winced. 'Why did I say that?'

Cherry regarded her keenly. 'You tell me. Was it in the dream?'

'I don't know. I never remember them clearly. Just feelings and faces – and a frightening man with a scar down his face and a crooked neck.'

'That would be the manservant, Mister Dark. People around here remembered him as a boogeyman long after it was all over. He must've been a real nasty customer. Anyway, this Melchior was creatin' an incredible magical device. The Nimius was going to be the new wonder of the age and whoever possessed it would have crazy, outtasight powers.'

'The Nimius?'

'You betcha. But somethin' went wrong. Annie and Melchior argued and died, and the Nimius was lost.'

'Not lost,' Lil murmured.

Cherry put her mug down.

'Personally, I never believed in the Nimius bit,' she said. 'I thought it was just a gimmicky late add-on, same as happens with every other myth. Boy, was I ever wrong. I just wish I knew where the heck on the West Cliff it is right now. Somebody's got it and they're usin' it.'

'How did Annie and her gentleman die?'

'Why don't you tell me?'

'How could I know?'

'Because, Lil, the skeleton that came flyin' through your window Friday night *was* Annie – leastways, what's left of her. They were her bones. The skull that's missin' was hers and the malevolent spirit that's possessin' you right now and listenin' to every word we say . . . that's hers too.'

Lil jolted upright. 'What?' she cried.

'That pickle-barrel witch has her hooks in you. Can't you feel it? Can't you sense her nastiness squattin' in your mind?'

The girl's hand moved to her throat. 'No – I can't!' she uttered.

'Then she ain't got a strong enough hold yet. I reckon you've held out far longer than she was expectin'. Perhaps there's still time to banish her. If we don't, you'll end up under her control completely and then you won't exist no more.'

Lil looked horrified and she began to twist something concealed under her jumper.

'You realise what you got there?' Cherry asked.

'What? Oh. I don't know.' Reaching under the neck of her jumper, Lil pulled out a dirty necklace of three ammonites.

'Where did this come from?' she spluttered. 'I've never seen this before!'

'Another thing you been blottin' out. It's been there since Friday night. Annie's skeleton must've put it there when you were unconscious.'

'How can you know that?'

Cherry held out her hand and showed Lil the bracelet set with three ammonites.

'They're the sign of the Whitby witch,' she told her. 'We've all had them. It's our badge of office. That necklace would have been Annie's.'

'But I'm not a witch.'

'You sure about that?'

'Course I am!'

'Honey, you've spent your whole life denyin' the existence of magic and by doin' that you've also been repressin' your true self, pushin' your natural talents way, way down. But you can't stifle that gift completely; it'll pop out in other kooky ways. Your knitting, for example.'

'It's just wool!'

'No it ain't, babe. You think you've been castin' on, but you've been castin' spells. When you put up your first lot of decorations the other day, I could sense there was a tingle of force in them. You were puttin' up defences, protectin' the East Cliff, without even knowin' it. I'm guessin' that's why Annie's had such a tough time dominatin' you, but that's probably why you were chosen in the first place, cos you're a young witch like she was.'

'Even if that was true, which it most definitely isn't, what does she want with me?'

'All I can say is a great power is out to destroy Whitby and it's resurrected the old feud between the ragged witch and the gentleman as the way to do it. Annie has been granted this second chance at revenge through you, while some poor sucker on the West Cliff is the selected vessel of Melchior Pyke. The two of you are gonna slug it out, bringin' an end to this town in the process. Sheesh, they must've hated one another real fierce for it to have lasted all these centuries beyond the grave.'

'But you can exorcise her though, right? Get rid of her?'

'Bell, book and candle ain't really my thing, but I'll give it my best shot. You don't want that dirty sack of bile and bitterness clutterin' up your psyche a minute longer. Beats me how anyone could have fallen for her in the first place. You wanna know how she died? A mob led by a Puritan called John Ashe hanged her and threw her body in a cesspit. Good riddance. She was an evil stain on this world.'

'Shows how much you know!' Lil snarled suddenly in a vicious, gargling voice that was not her own. 'And you won't rid this child of me. Her strength ain't no match for mine and your powers are puny. I got the might of the Three to draw on!'

Cherry leaned back in the wicker chair and it

swung gently on its chain as she stared at the horrible transformation taking place before her eyes.

Lil's face was rippling as a repulsive change stole over it. Her young features shrank against the bones of her skull. Her eyes sank into their sockets and her lips withered and turned black.

'Thought you was never gonna show yourself,' Cherry said with a bitter smile. 'Time us two had a girly chat. From one witch to another, I gotta tell you: this insane vendetta has to stop, right now. Let go of all that rage and anger and go find the peace you should've had when you died. Stop hauntin' this town and clear out of this girl's head. She's a good kid and done you no harm.'

'I will have my revenge,' the hate-filled voice spat from Lil's mouth. 'I have been promised. Whitby will pay.'

'OK,' Cherry said with a resigned sigh. 'Guess it was too much to expect you to do this the easy way. I need to understand what went on all them years ago. Budge up in there, sister, I'm comin' in.'

Cherry tore off her sunglasses and her pale eyes blazed out once more. A scream of protest issued from Lil's lips, then the girl's body slumped back, the walls of the cottage vanished and the centuries peeled away.

12

Cherry found herself standing in the Whitby of long ago. Church Street stretched before her as a long, narrow road of bare, stony earth, lined by ramshackle fishermen's cottages. It was a warm night in high summer, with a bright moon hanging low in the sky, and the inhabitants of the little town were tucked in their beds. Across the river, stripped of the clustering guesthouses and street lights, the West Cliff was a dark bank of shadow.

'Where are we?' a voice asked. 'It's like home but so different.'

Cherry smiled. A wide-eyed Lil was at her side. She was back to her usual self.

'Good to see ya, kid,' Cherry said. 'It's reassurin' that there's enough of you left to manifest an avatar here. Now don't be scared; we're inside your head. I just jumped in. It's kinda like my party piece.'

The girl grimaced and gazed around.

'This is my mind? It's not what I expected.'

'Yeah, well, it's your head, but it's not your mind. Scaur Annie's taken that over and we're standin' in one of her memories. I aimed for the night it all went sour, the night she died. This better be it.'

Before Lil could ask any more questions, they both heard desperate sobbing and turned to see the lone figure of a young woman stumbling along the street, from the direction of the shore.

'Must be Scaur Annie,' Cherry breathed. 'Well, I can honestly say she looks better in the flesh.'

'She was so young,' said Lil.

'I take it all back. That pickle-barrel stack of bones was a real babe.'

'Shouldn't we hide before she sees us?'

'This is a memory, honey, and we're just tourists. None of this is real; it already happened a long time ago. No one we meet can see or hear us. Think of it as being inside an old movie.'

'You sure? Seems very real to me. I can smell the sea and chimney smoke.'

'So she has a great memory. Now hush, I need to find out what happened here that night.'

As Annie drew near, they heard her cursing and reproaching herself.

'What have I done?' she wept. 'I betrayed them who was only ever good to me. A pestilence on my ungrateful head. They'll spit on my footprints in the sand and won't never speak to me no more and I don't blame 'em. The caves'll be shut against me from now on. Landbreed, that's what I am, hateful landbreed, never to be trusted. No different from the rest.'

She staggered to a halt and leaned against the wall of The White Horse inn, beating her fists against the stonework.

Cherry stepped closer warily. She was certain the young woman could not see her, but the intensity of Annie's anguish was unnerving.

The gulping sobs continued. Looking straight through Cherry, Annie stared back along the empty street and screwed her face up wretchedly. Then she turned to look up at a window of the inn where a lantern was burning.

'You did it for *him*,' she told herself. 'Aye, Annie, you faithless she-wolf. And you'd do it again if he asked. You'd do owt for his favour, rip out your soul and burn it, if that'd keep you near him. It's a blind madness in your blood and there ain't no cure.'

Blundering into the inn, she ran up the stairs.

'Come on, Lil,' Cherry called and they hurried after her.

Melchior Pyke was sitting at the table in his private parlour, poring over his books and writing in his journal, when Annie burst in on him.

'I done it!' she told him, her face burning with

shame. 'And may the Three punish me evermore for it! Here's proof for you!'

Holding out her hand, she put a small phial on one of the open pages.

Lil and Cherry stood in the doorway.

'I recognise this place from my dreams,' Lil whispered. 'And him.'

'Yeah, this is the big love story. He ain't bad-lookin' I suppose, but he sure is a dork in that big lacy collar.'

The man stared at the phial in wonder. The fluid it contained glimmered with a pale silver radiance.

'What is that?' Lil asked.

Cherry shrugged. 'No idea, but it must be mighty special judgin' by the state she's in.'

''Tis the proof you wanted,' Scaur Annie said. 'Take it.'

Melchior Pyke lifted the phial reverently and placed it in front of a candle flame, then viewed it through a magnifying lens.

'Is it truly the tears of Morgawrus?' he asked.

'That it is. Fresh from the sleeping serpent's eye. So you see, there are deep secrets in Whitby, old as the bones of the earth. I spoke truly. I wouldn't be false to my lordly gentleman.'

'Whoa!' Cherry declared. 'That's bigger than special. The serpent's tears? She's gotta be foolin'!'

'How could I have doubted you?' Melchior Pyke

was saying to Annie. 'If this precious liquid possesses the virtues I have searched so long for . . . its worth is immeasurable.'

'Cost me my heart's blood,' Annie told him. 'A price you won't never know nor understand and I won't never be rid of the guilt and shame of it.'

Melchior Pyke held the phial to his chest and bowed his head.

'So endeth the journey,' he whispered. 'The final element is found and all things shall be mine.'

Then he began to laugh, wildly, and he jumped up and embraced Annie, showering her with kisses.

'How can I repay you?' he asked. 'Thou rare, most wonderful creature.'

'Take me away,' she implored him. 'I can't stay here. Whitby's done with me. I don't belong no more. I've made a shipwreck of my life.'

'Whatever, wherever you wish. If you did but know the joy you have given me with this. I am versed in many languages, but in none of them are there fitting words to praise you or convey my gratitude.'

Annie pulled away from him.

'What I did don't deserve no praise,' she said. 'I should be whipped raw and sand rubbed rough in the welts. I'm the worst there ever were, worser than what anyone ever called me. Disgusting, that's what I am.'

'I must attend to this,' Melchior Pyke declared, examining the phial with the lens again and snatching up the quill. 'After this night, the world will never be the same, my dear.'

'Aye,' Annie said remorsefully. 'Changed for all that's bad and there's no road back.'

'Rabbit-brained witterings,' he answered. 'Such timorous qualms of conscience do you no service, my little gull charmer. Do not baulk now. There is a glorious golden future ahead. Be oak-hearted and iron-stomached; remember you are the fearless witch of Whitby.'

Annie shook her head and took a stumbling step away.

'Not no more,' she uttered. 'I overturned all that was right an' proper. I broke the ancient order.'

Shuddering, she hugged herself. She suddenly felt hemmed in and wanted to run and never stop. She had to get away from here.

'Come walk on the cliff, my love,' she urged him. 'I need the sea's breath to clear my head. Let us be together 'neath the stars again. Help me unburden my sorrow. Lift this heavy stone from my spirit.'

Melchior Pyke's quill continued to scratch across the pages of his journal as he drew strange symbols and made calculations.

'I beg you!' she cried.

'Mistress, can you not see I am occupied?'

Scaur Annie shied away as if he had struck her. Turning from him, she fled the room.

218

In the doorway, Cherry Cerise and Lil watched her go. Cherry threw Melchior Pyke an angry look.

'Was there *ever* a time in human history when guys understood women?' she asked, exasperated. 'Go after her, you dumb turkey!'

But Melchior Pyke could not hear her. Cherry gave a grunt of annoyance and hurried down the stairs with Lil. Some moments later, the nobleman raised his eyes from the esoteric signs and squiggles on the page. His brows furrowed, then he grinned.

'It is done,' he murmured.

Cherry and Lil were already running up the street to catch up with Scaur Annie. Leaving the inn behind, they approached the steps that ascended the cliff to the church. These were not stone, but old timbers in poor repair. Annie began the climb.

'I don't get it,' Cherry muttered. 'Where's the big feud? That tiff just now wouldn't make them enemies with a bitterness that lasts four hundred years. There must be more to it.'

'What was she beating herself up over?' Lil asked. 'And what was all that stuff about snake tears?'

'I told you how Whitby was built on the back of a gigantic sleeping serpent. Well, that's what those tears are from. But how in the heck did Annie manage to . . .?' Cherry turned away from the steps and looked down at the shore.

'She came from that way,' she said. 'The answer

has to be down there. Come on, Lil!'

'What about Annie?'

'We'll catch up later; this won't take long. She'll be weepin' and wailin' up there a while yet.'

'What if she throws herself off the cliff?' Lil said. 'This is the night she died.'

'No,' Cherry reminded her. 'Annie was hanged. Besides, she ain't filled with hate yet. There's still more to come. We got time.'

And so they hurried from the steps, passed further down the street between the fishermen's cottages, and scrambled on to the moonlit sands. Keeping close to the cliff wall, until it curved round to meet the rocks of the Scaur, they went as fast as they could. Then Cherry froze in her tracks.

'Oh man!' she exclaimed. 'Would ya look at that . . .'

Lil couldn't believe it. In the sheer cliff face above them, two huge stone doors were wide open.

'What is that?' she asked.

'The entrance to the hidden caves!' Cherry breathed. 'That there is a whole heap of awesome!'

'Hidden caves?'

'They don't exist in our time, kid, but back then . . . I never dared dream I'd ever see this.'

Picking her way over slippery black rocks, she gazed up at the great slabs of stone. In the space beyond a soft light was glimmering.

'Who's in there?' Lil asked. 'Do people live in them?'

'Not human people,' Cherry told her with a delighted expression.

'Then . . . what?'

'Aufwaders.'

Even if there hadn't been a ladder made from coarse rope and wooden slats hanging from the threshold, Cherry would have found some way to get up there.

'Aufwaders,' Lil repeated as they began to climb. 'Yes, I think I dreamed about one of them. What are they?'

'They're the fisherfolk,' Cherry explained, full of excitement. 'I told you once, remember? Real shy, supernatural gnome types who love the sea. They lived in this place we call Whitby since way before the first humans came. They taught us the lore of the sea, how to use nets, make boats – all that neat stuff. But man was greedy and suspicious and violent and so the aufwaders withdrew to the tunnels and secret ways and used enchantment to hide themselves, until only humans with second sight could see them. Eventually, they became just another of Whitby's legends, and the word aufwader was forgotten, or was muddled and turned into "Old Whaler".'

'There's nothing about them in any of my parents' books.'

'I got better books, honey. The old broad who lived in my cottage before me collected tons of cool stories about this town. You don't know the half of it.'

'So what happened to the aufwaders?'

Cherry had reached the cave and she helped pull Lil up the final rungs.

'Their numbers dwindled,' she told her, 'and the last tribe was removed from the land of humankind by the Lords of the Deep and Dark, and these doors were sealed forever. Don't ask me who the Lords of the Deep and Dark are; you don't wanna know.'

But Lil was too busy staring at the cave they were now standing in to ask anything. It was festooned with fishing nets. Small boats that might have been built for children were ranged about the walls, and crab pots and baskets decorated with shells were stacked beside them. Overhead were two beautifully wrought silver lamps shaped like fish and high above their white flames were the immense iron cogs and chains of the mechanism that operated the doors. Then Lil noticed a seated figure in a shadowy corner.

An aufwader.

He was no taller than an eight-year-old human, but his hands were wrinkled and browned by many years of salty gales and baking summers. He was wearing a dark blue gansey knitted with the pattern unique to his family. Lil assumed the creature was male because she could see white side whiskers sticking out from under

the broad brim of a sealskin hat that had slipped over his face.

'Will he be able to see us?' she asked Cherry, and was taken aback when she saw that the woman was dabbing her eyes and sniffling.

'Never thought I'd ever get to see one,' Cherry said huskily. 'But no, this is still Annie's memory. We're just nosy visitors, remember? He doesn't know we're here.'

'He's spark out anyway.'

Entranced, and fizzing with curiosity, Cherry crept closer, crouching to get a better view. The aufwader's aged face was scored by deep lines. She saw a long, bulbous nose and two fleshy ears, which were tufted with bristles at the tips. His large eyes were closed and his mouth was hanging open. Cherry frowned.

'That don't look like a natural sleep to me.'

Then she saw a wooden tankard lying on its side behind the stool. The dregs of a black, oily liquid had pooled inside.

'I got me a real bad feeling,' she said. 'Stick close, Lil.'

Rising, she took the girl's hand and they moved deeper into the cave, through an arch leading to the tunnels beyond. It was eerily silent. There was no one in any of the cosy dwellings they came across and Cherry's unease mounted. Lil didn't like it either. Then, passing through a sacking curtain, they found them – the aufwaders of Whitby.

Lil gasped and murmured. 'Now *this* is mirificus.'

It was the largest chamber they had seen so far. It was evidently where the separate tribes assembled for important meetings or to celebrate sacred festivals. Entering the cavern, Cherry and Lil saw that this had been one of those nights. A bonfire was still burning in the centre, a feast was spread on low stone tables and there were more aufwaders than Cherry could ever have dreamed of. But each and every one of them was lying on the floor.

'They can't all be asleep,' Lil said in a trembling voice. 'Are they dead?' Casting her gaze around, she looked on those remarkable faces. Their weather-beaten features possessed an unearthly beauty, filled with dignity and wisdom. The sea wives were dressed in their best. Shell combs tamed their sandy hair and their finest, shore-found treasures adorned them as necklaces or were fastened about their brows and wrists. The menfolk had brushed their wiry sideburns and brought out their fanciest pipes, not the everyday clay variety, but heirlooms of burnished wood, with large bowls, expertly carved, depicting family histories and ancestral heroes. Many had spiralling stems, or a secondary bowl, so that a delicious blend of different dried seaweeds could be enjoyed. Some of those precious pipes lay splintered beneath their owners.

'Do you think it was a celebration for the full moon?' Lil asked. 'There's all sorts of folk traditions in my mum's books about that. I guess fisherfolk would be extra keen on tides and stuff.'

As she stepped between the sprawled bodies, Lil thought it was the saddest sight she had ever seen. Beside each aufwader was a spilled drinking vessel.

'Same as the one at the entrance,' she said.

Cherry nodded. She knew what had happened.

'Annie drugged – or poisoned them. Oh dear Lords, did she kill them? Us witches were supposed to mediate and be a bridge between humans and the fisherfolk – protectin' everyone. Hell, Annie! You degraded the legacy of those brave women who went before you. Shame on you, girl, and all for what? So you could impress your doily-wearin' bozo boyfriend by stealin' some serpent's tears? That wasn't love; it was somethin' dark and obsessive and scary.'

'This one's breathing!' Lil exclaimed. 'So they're not dead, or at least not all of them. Oh, it's awful. Can't we do something to help?'

'We can't affect anything in a memory that ain't even ours, kid. Come on, I seen enough. Let's go find Annie, see what else happened that night.'

With a last lingering look at the fisherfolk, Lil followed Cherry from the cavern.

13

In the year 1618, the Norman-built stones of St Mary's looked pretty much the same as they did in Lil's own time. But the cemetery was different; the tall memorial cross to Caedmon was absent and there were far fewer graves. The headstones stood vertical and true and the inscriptions were crisply carved and legible.

After the climb up the steps, Lil was out of breath. This was a warm summer night, but she was feeling cold and a strange tiredness was creeping through her.

'How can I be so whacked when I'm not really here?' she asked. 'That doesn't make sense. My legs are aching and I'm shattered.'

'Mental strain,' Cherry told her. 'You're only here because your will is so strong. You're a stubborn gal, but the effort is takin' its toll and . . .'

'And Annie is getting more of a hold on the real me?'

Cherry nodded.

'How long have I got?'

'I don't know, honey. Just stay with me as long as you can.'

'What happens when I can't? Will I disappear forever?'

'Not if I can help it. Now let's go find that treacherous witch. There's gotta be something we can use to fight her. Don't give up hope.'

'There!' Lil said, pointing.

In the distance, the figure of Scaur Annie was striding purposefully along the headland, towards the cliff edge.

'She *is* going to jump!' Lil cried. 'The story was wrong!'

'No,' Cherry insisted. 'There's still too many pieces of the puzzle missin'. This doesn't end yet.'

Then they heard a strange, mewling cry. Glancing upwards, they saw a winged shape launch itself from the crenellated tower of the church. Against the starry heavens it was only a black silhouette and for a fleeting moment Cherry thought it was a squalbiter, but it was the wrong sort of weather for those creatures to be abroad.

'Looks like a cat, with bat wings,' she said. 'Even sounds like one. But that's not possible.'

'That thing was in my dream,' Lil said. 'It's horrific.'

The strange beast swooped over the graveyard and flew into Annie's path, beating its wings and hissing. The young witch yelled, fending it off with her hands.

Just then a shrill, whistled command issued from the deep shadows that spilled down over the church walls, making Lil and Cherry both start. The creature ceased its attack at once and flew up to perch on a tombstone.

Now a tall, alarming figure came swaggering out.

'Oh my gods!' Cherry breathed. 'Who the hell is that?'

'That's Mister Dark!' Lil gasped fearfully. 'Annie's scared of him.'

'I'm not surprised,' Cherry said. 'No wonder he became the local boogeyman. He looks like a walkin' corpse.'

The moonlight made Mister Dark's pale face more deathly than ever. With the unsteady lurch of a drunken man, and a half-empty bottle of brandy, he passed through the graveyard, towards Annie.

Cherry shivered. She could see shadows of death around him. Taking hold of Lil's hand again, they followed reluctantly.

'Keep your devil cat away from me!' Annie bawled.

Mister Dark gave a slurring laugh and rubbed his fingers together. Blue sparks crackled round them.

'Catesby!' he called. 'Here!'

There was a rush of leathery wings and a moment later the creature was sitting on his shoulder, nuzzling the silver staples in its skull against the arcs of energy that snapped between his fingers. Mister

Dark put the bottle between his teeth and glugged down several mouthfuls.

'Catesby remembers you,' he told Annie with a filthy wink.

'Your pet demon is a grey-fleshed evil that should have stayed dead,' she answered. 'Same as you!'

Mister Dark staggered closer.

'That's not courteous,' he said. 'You're polite enough and more to my lord. Me and Catesby are only out rat catching. Catesby likes hunting, loves to pounce and hear them squeak when he bites he does – and so do I.'

Smirking, he held out the bottle to her.

'Drink,' he said.

'Let me by! Or I'll report you to your master.'

The man guffawed and would have toppled backwards if he hadn't crashed against a headstone. Annie pulled a disgusted face and walked off.

'You think you're so important to him?' he called after her. 'Not no more you're not. Given him what he wanted, have you? That's you ended. He's sly as Old Nick. A better play actor I never did see.'

Annie turned.

'What's that you say?' she asked.

'I seen him get what he desired a score of times and more from folks who should know better. They always believe his honey promises. But you, you was the easiest of the lot. We both laughed about it. You

231

was starving for fair and flowery words he said, and he fed you right well.'

Annie glared at him.

'That's all you know!' she said angrily. 'There's love between us. He's going to take me with him. We'll live in his big house, down London way. In the summer, I'll eat frozen snow that tastes of roses.'

Mister Dark sneered at her. 'There is no big house,' he said. 'His lordship's got no fortune. He spent his estates journeying the world and buying rare books and gold and gems for his great work.'

'Jealousy and spite!' she snapped back. 'That's what this is. I won't listen.'

'You don't even know what his great work is,' Mister Dark scoffed. 'So much for love and trust. You mean no more to him than any mercer he owes a sovereign to, and there's many of them.'

'That's bile and bottle talk!'

''Tis the Bible truth and if you weren't so clod simple you'd know it. My master doesn't have enough jingle in his purse to pay his lodging this week and he still owes for his last. But now you've given him what he needed he'll be wealthier than all the kings and emperors put together. No more flea-ridden cots in outbuildings for Mister Dark. Goose-feather mattresses from now on and fat pigeons for Catesby whenever he wants, if he don't have a taste for juicier meat. Aye, merry times for us.'

The anger had drained from Scaur Annie's face as confusion and doubt took its place.

'How will the serpent's tears do so much?' she asked.

'Because that's the last element he needed for his grand masterpiece.'

'His great work? Tell me, what is it?'

Mister Dark gave a repulsive laugh.

''Twill be the marvel of the age!' he announced in a coarse imitation of Melchior Pyke's voice. 'My clever lord has poured all his cunning into its creation. Its power is beyond measure and will make him greater than any man in the known world. There was but one thing it lacked: the perfect fluid to drive its tiny engine. And so his book learning brought him hither, to this dirty town.'

'How can that be? He knew nothing of Morgawrus till I told him! He didn't even believe me. I had to furnish proof.'

'Wake up! He knew everything! About that – and about them little leathery-faced skulkers who guard it. But Pykey don't have the sight, see, so it was Mister Dark's job to seek them out and get the tears from them. Alas, those crab lovers didn't fancy the looks of me, so another way had to be found, and that were you. It didn't take his lordship long to charm Whitby's wild witch.'

'A tower of lies! He saved me from the mob's flames.'

Mister Dark guffawed unpleasantly. 'And why was they at your door that night?' he asked. 'Cos a few sheep had been killed where you'd been seen. Who do you think had your journeys watched and ordered them sheep dead? What do you think killed them fat bleaters? Catesby liked his bit of mutton, didn't you? Not so partial to rats as he once was. Spoiled him it did. Got a real taste for their red juices; made him feel young and strong. Should've seen the lustre of his coat after.'

Annie stepped away from him, her face almost as pale as his own.

'My fine gentleman used me,' she said in stunned realisation. 'I been played from start to finish. I betrayed my lovely fisherfolk for a basketful of falsehoods.'

Mister Dark wiped his mouth on his hand. 'You might profit by it yet,' he told her. 'From now on, gold will stick to him like pig muck to a boot. He might fling some coins your way if you carry on being so polite.'

Annie wasn't listening. Her face had set grim and hard and she strode through the graveyard back towards the steps. Grasses and plants that brushed her skirt as she stormed by blackened and died and thunder rolled overhead though the sky was clear.

*

Cherry and Lil had watched the whole exchange in silence.

'So that's what did it,' said Lil at last. 'That's what turned Annie's love to hate.'

'When a passion so all-consumin' goes bad,' Cherry said, 'the hatred is overwhelmin', unhinged – frightenin'.'

'She's going to see Pyke now, isn't she?'

'Yeah, and it won't be pretty. You sure you want to witness it?'

'Nothing could stop me. We've come this far.'

'Yes, go watch,' came a sneering voice. 'Go see the final confrontation between the broken-hearted witch and her false gentleman.'

Cherry and Lil stared at each other, then looked at the speaker. To their bewilderment and horror they saw that Mister Dark was looking straight at them.

'Oh yes,' he said. 'Catesby and me can see and hear you both. Thought you could slink about unnoticed, did you? Prying into dusty corners, like invisible little mice, looking for a way to avert the oncoming doom?'

'That's impossible!' Cherry spluttered. 'This is just a memory! These events happened centuries ago. You're long dead. There's no way you can be aware of us.'

'And yet I am,' the man said with a filthy leer. Straightening, he threw the bottle away and he no

235

longer appeared drunk. On his shoulder, Catesby hissed at Cherry and the girl.

'You think Annie and Pyke are the only ones with a footing in your time?' he asked. 'The Lords of the Deep and Dark can do anything. Them under the sea have many schemes and many agents. Some are more trusted than others; some have special commissions. They're not going to allow the likes of you to foul their plans. This squalid little town is about to feel the full force of their fury and there's nothing a paltry colour witch can do to stop it. Nothing.'

He raised his hand and rubbed his fingers together. Catesby bathed its grotesque head in the resulting sparks.

'Run,' he told them. 'Go observe the final act. Your own deaths are snapping at your heels. The girl is fading fast. She has but moments left before her mind, her life, all that she was, is snuffed out like a candle.'

Lil backed away and Cherry gripped her hand. It was deathly cold.

'Don't listen to him!' Cherry cried fiercely. 'Don't believe him. I've got tight hold and I won't let go. You stay with me, Lil Wilson. We're gonna follow Annie. There might still be a chance, something I can do.'

With Mister Dark's mocking laughter ringing in their ears they ran for the steps. Cherry tried not to let her fear show, but she was mortally afraid. The malevolence within that sinister man was greater than anything she had ever encountered.

'Your pitiable colour magic is no match for the power of dark,' he called after them. 'All shall die!'

Lil was gasping when they reached the steps. 'I . . . I have to stop and rest.'

'No time for that!' Cherry told her. 'Come on, one last dash to the inn.'

'I can't,' Lil sobbed, sinking to her knees. 'I'm too weak.'

'Don't give up!' Cherry pleaded, rubbing her icy hand. 'Just hang in there a little longer. You can do it!'

Lil stared up at her, her eyes dim and dying. 'Tell Verne I'm sorry,' she said.

Shadows gathered round her. Then, to Cherry's horror, Lil crackled and vanished.

'No!' Cherry cried. 'No!'

Above her, the night was filled with the mewling of Mister Dark's repugnant pet as Catesby flew high over the clifftop.

Trembling with shock and grief, Cherry stared back at the graveyard. Mister Dark was approaching, a cruel smile on his scarred face.

'In your world,' he said, 'Annie's vengeful spirit now has complete control of that girl's mindless body. At this very moment she is leaving your cottage to bring about Whitby's ultimate ruin. Why do you tarry here in this sordid memory? If you hurry you might just escape the violence she is about to unleash. But you'd better be quick – there's so little time before the drowning darkness comes.'

Cherry turned away and began running down the wooden steps.

'Not yet, buster!' she shouted. 'I'm seeing this tragedy through to its bitter end. If I'm the last witch of Whitby, then that's my job. Besides, I owe it to Lil.'

Reaching the top of the steps, Mister Dark observed her descent. A scowl gouged deep grooves into his pallid forehead. Putting his tongue against the back of his teeth, he whistled a command to Catesby and the creature flew after her.

At The White Horse, Scaur Annie threw open the door of the private parlour, only to find it empty.

'Where is he?' she snapped when a curious Mary Sneaton appeared on the landing, bearing a candle.

'What uproar is this?' the landlord's daughter demanded. 'I thought robbers had broke in.'

'Where is the lord of deceit?'

'His lordship is most likely in the outbuilding. He often keeps ungodly hours in there at his labours.'

'His labours!' Annie spat in contempt as she pushed past her and Mary was alarmed to see the cold fury in her eyes.

'What has occurred?' she called. 'Annie, what is it?'

But the young witch was already through the door and marching across the stable yard.

In the workshop, Melchior Pyke leaned back and surveyed the treasure in his hands. It was the most ravishing object he had ever seen, the crowning achievement of his life. He had made so many sacrifices to reach this glorious moment, but they had been worth it. His fingertips caressed the scrolling gold lovingly, touching the many symbols on its glittering surface.

'What shall be the first trial?' he asked. 'What wonder will I bid it to perform?'

It was then the door swung open and Annie stood on the threshold. She stared at the golden object in his hands.

'What have you there, my love?' she asked.

Melchior Pyke was so enamoured of his great work he did not notice the steel in her voice.

'You cannot begin to imagine,' he said proudly.

'Tell me.'

'It is that which has consumed thirteen years of my life. It is the embodiment of all the secret knowledge of the ancients. This is my great work that you so desired to see. Is it not magnificent? See how the lantern light dances and flares over it. But the greatest wonders are concealed within.'

'Are the serpent's tears in there?'

'How clever you are. Yes, that was all it lacked. Now it is done – is it not the most beguiling prize under heaven?'

'It looks like a golden heart.'

The man laughed. 'It is the hazelnut of wisdom and inspiration,' he corrected. 'But yes, if viewed the other way, it could resemble a heart. And what could be more fitting? A passion greater than love has gone into its making.'

'You have made a cold, hard heart.'

'There is fire within, I assure you. This miracle is now capable of performing unbelievable feats. Nations would wage war to possess it, but only he who wields this glittering thing would be victorious. No enemy could withstand its power. And see, here, behold the word I have this very hour inscribed upon its ravishing surface.'

Annie stepped into the workshop.

In the yard outside, Cherry Cerise had finally caught up with her. She saw the young witch enter the outbuilding and dashed after.

Wrapped in a deadly, glacial calm, Annie gazed down at the word cut into the precious metal.

'What does it say?' she asked. 'I do not know my letters. You were going to teach me, my love.'

'So I was, but no matter. I had always intended to engrave the Greek word *Kallisté*, which in antique myth was written upon the apple of discord and means *most beautiful*. But that is no longer adequate.'

'What then have you written?'

'Nimius!'

240

'What does that mean? I am but an ignorant witch of this dirty town called Whitby. Here, let me pour you some wine. This is a moment of celebration, is it not?'

'No moment more worthy,' he agreed. 'We must make a toast, to the pinnacle of my endeavours! The word Nimius means *beyond measure*. It could not be more appropriate.'

'Then Mister Dark spoke truly,' she said.

'What does that surly villain know of it?' he snorted.

'Enough to bring me back here, one last time.'

Cherry watched Annie take a jug from the shelf. Melchior Pyke was too engrossed in gazing at the Nimius to see her slip a small bottle from her sleeve and tip the black contents into the wine.

''Tis a night for toasts,' Annie said, swilling the liquid round the jug before pouring it into two goblets. 'This shall be the second that Annie has overseen, but this one she shall relish far more. Here, my lord. To your Nimius and a golden future.'

Unable to take his eyes off the gleaming treasure, Melchior Pyke drained the goblet.

'To the glory that is the Nimius,' he said, not noticing she hadn't touched any of her own wine. 'The word flew into my head whilst I was making my final . . . calculations. As . . . soon as . . .'

He coughed and cleared his throat. 'The wine

burns strangely,' he said. 'I feel . . . I am unwell. A sharp tightness across the chest. Agh, there is a fire in my veins!'

'Two drops for sleep,' Annie told him. 'Six for death. I betrayed my true friends, the aufwaders, with two drops. But you, my love, have had the whole bottle.'

'What?' his voice rasped. 'What have you done?'

'Here at the very instant of your triumph,' she spat. 'The ragged witch of Whitby denies you its sweetness. You shall not break another girl's heart.'

Melchior Pyke's eyes filled with terror and black bile spilled from his lips. With the Nimius still clutched in his hand, he crashed to the floor.

'Retch your way to the grave, m'lord,' she said. 'And take my undying curse with you! May you find neither rest nor peace.'

'Nimius!' his gargling voice gasped as he died at her feet. 'Nimius . . .'

Standing by the door, Cherry closed her eyes and turned away. But the horrors were not over yet.

Above the stable yard sounded an unmistakable mewling cry.

'Catesby!' Annie said, jerking her head around. 'Then Mister Dark will be close behind! He must not get the Nimius. None must have it! 'Tis too mighty a thing. It must be hid!'

Crouching, she tried to take the Nimius from the

dead man's hand. But Melchior Pyke's fingers gripped it like a vice. The poison had locked them rigid. She could not wrench it free. Outside, Catesby's wailing cry sounded once more and she heard footsteps hurrying into the yard. There was only one thing to do.

She reached across the workbench and snatched a hacksaw from the ordered array of tools. In her haste she knocked over a large jar of sulphur. The glass shattered and great quantities of yellow powder spilled out.

'Dear Lords!' Cherry exclaimed when she saw what Annie did next.

Within moments Scaur Annie had cut the hand off at the wrist. Carrying it and the Nimius she fled the workshop – and ran into Mary Sneaton.

'Is all well?' the innkeeper's daughter asked. 'I thought I heard our Catesby. Has he come back? He doesn't sound too good. Annie! What is that you ha–?'

Mary screamed when she realised what the young witch was carrying. Annie pushed her aside and fled into the street. Mary stared after her, then turned to the open door of the workshop. Soon she was screaming again.

'Help! Murder!' she screeched, racing into the inn to rouse her father. 'Murder! She's killed his lordship!'

In the workshop, Cherry Cerise shook her head. Everything was clear to her now.

'Annie will bury the Nimius up on the cliff

someplace,' she murmured. 'And it'll stay hid for four hundred years. Accordin' to the story, just before dawn John Ashe and his rabble will find Annie stumblin' along the lanes. He'll drag her to Sandsend and they'll hang her from a tree. This is how hatred endures beyond the grave.'

Utterly beaten, Cherry knew it was time to leave this harrowing memory and return to her own time. It had been a wasted effort. She had learned nothing that could help save Whitby and it was too late to try. Casting a final despairing glance around the workshop she prepared to leave.

Then something on the bench caught her eye. It was Melchior Pyke's journal. The book lay open and Cherry bent over it to read the last words he had written. 'Oh brother!' she cried as she stared at the pages. 'That's it! That's the answer!'

'An answer that must remain unspoken,' a threatening voice said behind her.

Cherry turned to see Mister Dark standing in the doorway, with Catesby on his shoulder.

'You!' Cherry shouted. 'All of this is your doing! You want the Nimius for yourself, don't you?'

'Of course,' he said with an ugly smile. 'Who would not want to possess the marvel of this or any other age? He who operates it has the power of a god. It will be mine; it has been promised. When Whitby lies beneath the cold waves, the Nimius will be given unto me. A fresh young life is already waiting so that I may live again.'

Cherry shook her head. 'No,' she said defiantly. 'I'm gonna end this right now.' Her eyes blazed blue and she willed herself out of this nightmarish memory, back into her own cottage.

'I told you, you are no match for the power of dark.'

Cherry uttered a horrified gasp. She was unable to leave the workshop. 'I've trapped you here,' the manservant said, closing the door behind him as he stepped closer. 'What a pity there are no bright colours in this drab outbuilding to give your petty powers a little boost. But then you're better off here. The Whitby of your time has only a few minutes left. The warring spirits of Annie and Pyke will make the people of the two cliffs annihilate one another, and then the sea shall roar in to destroy what remains. Your real body won't feel any pain. You won't know when the monstrous waves come crashing into your cottage; you'll simply blink out of existence, the same as that child did. You should thank me really.'

He began to laugh, a horrible taunting laugh. Cherry stepped away from him. Then a desperate idea came to her.

'I hope that Nimius is good at Botox,' she said, 'cos you sure need a whole heap of work on that ugly mug of yours, sweetheart. What's the point of being all powerful if you've got a face that would scare a gargoyle? Not gonna look good on the stamps of your new empire, is it? Who's gonna want to lick them? Dark really is the best place for you; no one should have to see that mush in the daylight. And that pet of yours ain't gonna win no best-in-show rosettes neither. They'll have to invent new names for that freaky feline – it's not a pretty kitty. Meow Monster, that's what they'll call it, or Frankenpuss. Yeah, Frankenpuss, that's the one.'

Taunting it with jerky hand movements and barking like a dog, she hopped from side to side, giving the craziest, most antagonising performance of her life.

On Mister Dark's shoulder, Catesby hissed and flexed its claws. Then it flew at her in a rage. Cherry kept close to the bench as the creature dived, slashing at her and spitting, the leathery wings beating furiously.

'Call it off!' Cherry begged. 'I'm sorry! Call it off!'

Mister Dark's scarred lip curled unpleasantly as he grinned. He let Catesby harry her some moments more, then whistled a command and rubbed his fingers together. The sparks crackled around them.

Too late, he realised how Cherry had tricked him. The air was now filled with clouds of sulphur dust, sent swirling by Catesby's wings, and the sparks from his fingers ignited it.

There was an ear-splitting explosion and the outbuilding was blown apart. The chemicals stored in the workshop erupted in flames of different brilliant colours.

Cherry yelled out and leaped back. She fell against the wicker chair hanging from her ceiling and knocked over her green tea that was now cold. Her mind was back in her body, inside her cottage.

Breathing hard, she stared at the chaise longue. It was empty and the front door was wide open.

14

The moment Lil's exhausted mind vanished from the memory of that fateful night, Scaur Annie's spirit was in complete control. The possessed girl left Cherry's cottage, and made straight for the Wilsons'. Once there she entered Lil's room and stood before the dresser mirror. The reflection bulged and the skull came floating from the undulating glass. It drifted forward and the jaw swung open. The long, wet hair churned thickly as if caught in an infernal breeze. It wrapped tightly about the girl's head and the old bones merged with the girl's living flesh. The skin that was already withered turned paper-thin and the sunken eyes were red-rimmed and staring. It was a horrific, loathsome sight.

'The hour is upon us,' Annie's voice declared.

On the bed, Sally's nose began to twitch and the little dog awoke. Her milky eyes peered at the frightful apparition before her. Although it was wearing Lil's clothes, it reeked of the grave. The Westie began to bark, frantic and frightened.

Scaur Annie ignored her and left the bedroom. It was time for the climactic battle between the ragged witch and the despicable scholar who had deceived her, Sir Melchior Pyke. But this time they would not face one another alone.

'Step forth,' she called as she descended the Wilsons' stairs. 'Step forth. You are all Whitby witches now!'

Mr and Mrs Wilson emerged from their bedroom, cloaked and wearing white make-up on their blank faces. In obedient, spellbound silence they followed her. Sally barked as never before.

The skull-faced girl strode up Henrietta Street, summoning the residents from their beds. Every person was wearing dramatic gothic make up and had backcombed hair, even the children and the pensioners, and those without genuine cloaks had torn down curtains and cut up duvet covers to make them.

At the bottom of the 199 steps, Scaur Annie halted. She raised a skeletal hand and cried out.

'Join us!'

Dawn was breaking. Darkness was giving way to a leaden half-light and a blanket of mist lay over the ancient churchyard. At Annie's summons, the graves burst open and withered corpses clambered up into the chill air. Stretching their creaking joints and cracking their soil-fused spines, they came down the steps, a cascade of marching bones, and the mist flowed with them.

Annie continued into Church Street. Every door she passed was pulled open and the inhabitants of the East Cliff swelled the ranks of her army as they made their way towards the swing bridge.

Verne was standing on the quayside of the West Cliff, wearing one of Clarke's crash helmets. It was criss-crossed with electrical wires and cogs and the Nimius had been attached to the front, ensuring the link with Melchior Pyke could not be broken. Verne's true personality and will were utterly crushed and under his domination.

The boy's family stood alongside him. Impeccably coiffured and manicured, his mother was dressed in her steampunk gear, fully working proton blaster at the ready. Mr Thistlewood was making final adjustments to a flame-thrower fitted to the Vespa and Clarke was kitted out in protective clothing, ready to ride across the bridge. With them, thronging the quayside and the roads that led down to it, was the entire population of the West Cliff. Each of them had brought something built under the influence of the Nimius. But this time there were no whimsical devices, only weapons. There were missile launchers made from drainpipes and old cookers, bazookas that used to be exhaust pipes and microwaves, which now fired plasma grenades. An array of robots, from small toasters that trundled along the ground on baby-buggy wheels to human-sized contraptions made from items scavenged from sheds and garages, formed two ranks either side of the bridge. In their midst was a hulking, five-metre-tall tank commando made from a converted minibus, with headlamp eyes and rockets on its wide shoulders.

Somewhere in that huge, expectant crowd, Jack Potts led a convoy of ambulatory tea urns and cake trolleys, dispensing refreshment to all who required it.

The forces of the West Cliff were ready. Usually at this hour the air would be teeming with squawking gulls, but not today. They remained on their roosts to watch the unnatural morning unfold. When one flew out incautiously, someone in the crowd aimed a particle pistol; a green ray shot up and the gull fell to the ground, roasted to perfection.

Sailing high overhead above the harbour was a two-man airship with a tin-bath gondola, armed with an automatic blunderbuss. When it sighted the enemy advancing through the East Cliff, it signalled the approach with a trumpet blast.

All eyes and brass goggles fixed upon the east side of the bridge. Jack Potts ceased pouring tea and waited, sugar tongs poised.

Verne took up a megaphone, but the voice that

issued from his lips was that of Sir Melchior Pyke.

'We must not fail this day,' he addressed the West Cliff. 'The ragged witch would have this world dragged back into ignorance. She would extinguish the bright flame of science and replace it with the old ways of spell casting and augury.'

Angry cries erupted around the quayside.

'She is driven by malice,' Melchior Pyke continued. 'A foul, black-hearted murderess. We cannot let her rise again. Her vicious evil must not take root and flourish. Our cause is righteous. We fight for liberty and learning. The day of the witch is dead. It is our solemn duty to ensure no man ever has to fear the darkness again. We are soldiers of the light, champions of enlightenment. Reason shall never be vanquished by hate and superstition!'

The crowd cheered with approval and then roared with anger when Scaur Annie and her army came into view across the river, as they strode down Bridge Street.

'Seal off the town!' Melchior Pyke instructed. 'Let no outsider enter!'

At that command, Mr Thistlewood raised a phase gun and discharged a short blast of violet energy that boiled through the sky. It was the signal for a series of deflectors made from satellite dishes and kitchen appliances positioned on rooftops around the West Cliff to be activated.

253

The air crackled with electricity as an arc of impenetrable force formed around that half of Whitby.

'Now let the ragged witch face us,' Melchior Pyke said, making Verne lower the megaphone and turn to the east side.

Scaur Annie led her legion of followers to the bridge. Immediately behind her was the host of skeletons from the graveyard, and hot on their heels were the residents she had summoned from their beds. Grey mist surged about them and curled around Annie.

'Let none pass into this place!' she commanded.

The clouds over the abbey began to curdle and

spread. They sank over the ruins and rolled out across the cliff, becoming a wall of dense fog that smothered the roads, cutting the town off from the eastern approach. Thunder shook the ground. Overhead, the dawn sky became black and spiked with lightning.

Annie stepped on to the bridge. On the other side, Verne did the same. Slowly, they advanced towards each other.

'Melchior Pyke!' she called out. 'Long ago I halted your ambition. This day I shall do so again. The Nimius will be wrested from you a final time!'

'Never!' he shouted back. 'There is no power equal

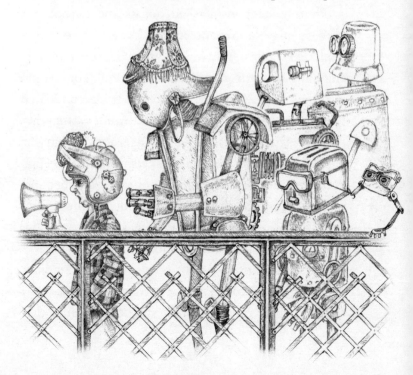

to that of my glorious creation. Your struggles are in vain.'

Annie turned to her followers.

'Wake the storm!' she commanded.

The inhabitants of the East Cliff began to chant. Their combined voices resonated through the air. At once a stiff gale came gusting through the cobbled streets and went blasting across the harbour. The smaller robots were knocked over, many in the crowd were thrown off their feet and top hats went flying into the distance.

'In the name of science,' Melchior Pyke yelled, 'let battle commence!'

Photon weapons flashed across the harbour. A glowing plasma grenade crackled over the river and exploded against the wall of the *Gazette* building, engulfing it in turquoise flame. The tank-commando machine came stomping on to the bridge and fired two rockets from its shoulders. Annie raised her hands. Jagged forks of lightning erupted from the clouds and detonated the rockets in mid-air. High above, riding the buffeting wind, the airship pilots took aim with the automatic blunderbuss and fired into the enemy below. The shots went wild, ricocheting off the pantile roofs.

Annie let loose a shrill, screeching cry. At once, five squalbiters came racing through the sky. They clamped their claws into the stitched cagoules that formed the airship's inflated gas bag and began slashing and tearing. The dirigible spun out of control, losing height until it splashed into the river.

The host of robots went clanking across the bridge. Screaming, the skeletons rushed to meet them. The clamour of war was deafening.

Cherry Cerise came rushing through the narrow streets, pushing past her neighbours. In their gothic make-up and witchy attire she barely recognised them. But there wasn't time to stare at their transformation. Photon bolts were slicing the air above their heads and several shop awnings were already ablaze. Soon there would be serious casualties, then deaths and carnage. Dodging between the crowds, she squeezed her way to the bridge.

The spectacle before her was insane and impossible. Not only was Whitby at war, so were the laws of nature and physics. Gritting her teeth, Cherry ploughed on through the chaos.

A thunderclap cracked overhead so loud she felt it boom in her chest, and Cherry cried out when she stared beyond the harbour piers at the horizon. A mountainous wave was forming. It was already higher than the topmost stone of the abbey.

Terrified, Cherry plunged further on to the overcrowded bridge. She could see Annie a little way ahead, close to the halfway point. She was surrounded by a vanguard of corpses, which were locked in a violent fight against the robots. Bones were being smashed and metal heads were tumbling into the river. All around, the storm howled and the dazzling beams of ray guns flared.

'Annie!' Cherry shouted urgently. 'You must listen to me! You have to stop this!'

The grotesque skull face upon Lil's shoulders regarded her with scorn as she strove to get closer.

'Why are you still here?' Annie asked.

'Because you need to know you were wrong!'

'You waste your final moments. I will have my revenge.'

'Mister Dark lied to you!' Cherry yelled.

The hideous face turned away and glared through the violent tangle of skeleton and robot warriors that fought between her and her enemy.

Verne's face was just as grim and determined. Melchior Pyke was deploying every weapon he had. When the mechanical devices had been spent, he would send in the human troops and ensure they fought to the death.

Cherry read that callous intent on both of their faces.

'It was Mister Dark!' she shouted again. 'He lied to you both. He was an agent of the Lords of the Deep. He wanted the Nimius for himself.'

Annie glared at her. 'Melchior Pyke used me!' she insisted.

'OK, so he used you to get the serpent's tears, but he loved you. Lords' sakes, he adored you, and if you hadn't listened to Mister Dark's lies you'd have known just how much. Melchior tried to tell you, for cryin' out loud!'

'This is a new lie of your own.'

'By my witch's oath I swear to you – and I can prove it! I saw what he wrote in his journal. Just search that memory one more time and see for yourself.'

The ghastly red-rimmed eyes stared at her uncertainly. 'Annie cannot read,' she said.

'But you know a girl who can!' Cherry answered. 'Lilith Wilson – the girl you've possessed. If there's a tiny echo of her mind left in there, use that, or bring her back if you can. Please! For all our sakes. Use that smart girl's brains and read that journal for yourself. Do it! Now!'

Papery skin closed over those bloodshot eyes.

The din of the battle was silenced and Scaur Annie was back in the workshop that fateful night.

''Tis is a night for toasts,' she was saying, pouring the contents of the poisoned jug into two goblets. 'This shall be the second that Annie has overseen, but this one she shall relish far more. Here, my lord. To your Nimius and a golden future.'

Melchior Pyke drank the wine in one thirsty draught.

'To the glory that is the Nimius,' he declared. 'The word flew into my head whilst I was making my . . . final . . . calculat . . .'

The deadly moment slowed to a stop and Annie stared hard at the open journal. But the funny squiggles still made no sense. She gave a cry of frustration and despair.

'I feel weird,' a young voice said abruptly. 'It's so cold. Am I dead?'

Annie turned and there was Lil, blinking and gazing around her.

'We both are, child,' Annie replied. 'But a wisp of your wits remains. Would you . . . would you aid me and read what is scribed there?'

'You want me to help you? After what you've done?'

'I do but ask it. I cannot compel you. Yet it would be a great kindness.'

'Can't you read?'

'No, and those words hold a terror for me.'

Lil saw the fear on Annie's face and, in spite of everything, she felt sorry for the witch.

'Let's have a look then,' she said gently.

Lil began to read, speaking the last written words of Sir Melchior Pyke out loud.

As I tarry for my true love's return, I am consumed with shame. I have used her most cruelly. The desire to complete my life's work had rendered me blind and log-headed and I must spend every day begging her forgiveness. This thing I have made is without parallel, but it is not fairer than she. It cannot bring me the same deep joy as her honest affection. Though it is wrought of gold, she is the one true prize of my life.

'Kallisté' was to be its name, but my own sweet dove is 'the most beautiful'. Therefore, I will call it Nimius and give it to her as a token of my enslavement, if she will forgive my folly. My love for Scaur Annie, that wild, ragged witch of Whitby town, truly is 'beyond measure' . . .

There was a tear in her eye when Lil looked up from the page.

'He named it for you,' she said. '"Nimius" is the word for how much he loved you. It's a big golden Valentine.'

Annie stared back at her. The enormity of what she had done was graven on her face.

Lil pitied her more than ever, but before she could say any more, the girl faded and was gone.

'The wine burns strangely,' Melchior Pyke said as the frozen moment thawed. 'I feel . . . I am unwell. A sharp tightness across the chest. Agh, there is a fire in my veins!'

*

Annie's scream of anguish catapulted her back to the bridge, where the battle was still raging. The animated corpses were almost beaten. They were no match for metal fighters and only one remained standing. The rest were heaped in severed pieces across the road and railings.

'Stop!' Annie shrieked. 'Stop!'

The chanting ceased. The last skeleton staggered back to look at her and a robot fist crunched clean through it.

'I was wrong!' Annie cried. 'I was wrong!'

The pain in her voice cut through the squalling wind and even the robots stood still.

Trembling, Annie stepped forward. She glanced nervously at Cherry and the colour witch nodded encouragement.

'My lord?' Annie called. 'My fine, noble gentleman. Scaur Annie knows now. She knows how much you loved her.'

The robots parted to let her through. Verne came closer. The storm clouds finally burst, the rain began lashing down and Cherry shielded her eyes. The figures on the bridge were transformed. A beautiful young woman in a ragged gown and bare feet was standing before a handsome man in a velvet doublet with a white lace collar.

'Why did you doubt me?' he asked.

'I told you,' she said, daring to raise the ghost of

a playful smile. 'I am just a common, ignorant witch girl.'

'You were never that. But you meant the world and more to me.'

'And you to me. I should have trusted my heart.'

'Don't waste any more time blaming yourselves,' Cherry told them. 'It was that lying reptile of a manservant. All of this misery was his doing.'

'Mister Dark?' Melchior Pyke muttered in dismay.

'You betcha. He was working for a different set of Lords entirely and dark was the power they gave him.'

'Is it over now?' Annie asked. 'Are we free of that foul wretch?'

Cherry shook her head. 'I can only hope.' she answered. 'Can dark ever be truly defeated? I dunno.'

'And what of us?' Melchior Pyke asked. 'Can we end four centuries of hate? I am so weary of it.'

'How can I be forgiven?' Annie wept.

'Holy salamis on a pogo stick!' Cherry declared impatiently. 'Just kiss and make up!'

'One should always pay heed to the Whitby witch,' Melchior Pyke said. Taking Annie in his arms, he kissed her full on the lips.

The air shook and a closing peal of thunder echoed over the harbour.

With that, the enchantment of the Nimius faltered. The robots and the rest of the impossible, preposterous machinery reverted to useless junk and started to fall apart. The energy shield around the West Cliff vanished and the people on the quayside awoke from their trances, astonished to find themselves out of doors wearing steampunk gear and wondering why home-made ray guns and other silly weapons were dropping to pieces in their hands.

On the East Cliff, a fresh wind blew the fog from the roads and the residents of the old part of town were aghast to find themselves heavily made up and wearing their best curtains.

Cherry gazed out to sea. The cataclysmic wave had disappeared. She let out a huge, thankful sigh and bowed her head.

'You didn't get us this time,' she breathed with relief. 'Not this time. But oh brother, it was close.'

'What are you doing?' a familiar but outraged voice was crying. 'Get off! Agh!'

Cherry spun round in time to see a very much alive Lil Wilson pushing Verne away.

'Hey!' Verne protested, spluttering and wiping his lips with equal distaste. 'What's going on? What you kissing me for?'

He stared around them and his eyes widened when he saw the piles of scrap and countless ancient battered bones.

'Another zombie apocalypse!' he exclaimed. 'And I missed it again!'

Then he became aware of the heavy crash helmet on his head and fumbled to remove it.

'Hey, kiddo,' Cherry greeted Lil warmly. 'Glad to have you back. And good to finally meet the kissy-kissy boyfriend.'

'He is not my boyfriend!' Lil answered emphatically before throwing her arms around Cherry and thanking her.

'No, honey,' Cherry said. 'We all need to thank *you*. You're the one that saved the whole damn town. You're the one who gave Annie and her gentleman their everlasting peace and I'm gonna make sure they all know about it.'

Lil had so many questions she didn't know where to begin. Then she saw her parents rushing towards her from the confused and startled crowd and she raced to hug them.

Moments later she was running again. A terrible, sickening thought had seized her. She splashed though the cobbled streets, desperate to get home.

Up on the West Cliff, standing beneath the whalebone arch, within the seal of the Lords of the Deep and Dark that she had painstakingly chalked on the ground, Tracy Evans uttered a howl of dismay. From that vantage point, she had been cheering the battle on with the foulest language, willing it to be over so that her beloved dream boyfriend could join her. But now everything was ruined. The destruction of Whitby had been averted and Tracy took out her phone to send desperate texts.

There was no reply.

Tracy yelled and screamed. She kicked the base of the nearest whalebone. Then she glared at the cheerful knitted sleeve that covered it and reached out with her fingernails to rip it to shreds.

The instant she touched it, a blast of energy hurled her backwards. Sprawled on the ground, her upturned face battered by the rain, she began sobbing.

'Where are you, Dark? Don't leave me on my own. I need you. What am I going to do now? Please come back to me.'

As she lay there, a cold shadow spread around her like a puddle and the silhouette of a hand stroked her pale, wet throat.

Tracy's tears turned to ugly laughter.

As she neared home, Lil's dread mounted. The front door was open. Breathing hard, she entered and sank to her knees.

What she feared had happened. The safety gate had not been put in place at the top of the stairs. Sally was lying at the bottom. Lil pressed her face against the Westie's head.

When the Wilsons returned, they found her in the hall, with the little dog's body in her arms.

'It's not fair,' Lil uttered desolately. 'After everything that's happened – it's not fair!'

Outside, the rain continued to fall.

GONGOOZLING

It was a gorgeous day and Cherry Cerise was wearing her favourite outfit: fuchsia wig, orange sombrero, pea-green blouse that also served as a miniskirt, fluorescent yellow leggings and raspberry vinyl knee-length platform boots. Her enormous sunglasses had retro, space-age silver frames.

Barging into the Wilsons' cottage, she stomped up the stairs and breezed into Lil's bedroom.

'Right, kid,' she said briskly. 'Today's the day you haul your sorry tushy outta here. It's glorious out there.'

Lil was still in bed, facing the wall.

Three weeks had passed. Lil had blamed herself for Sally's death. It rained all day and night, but Lil had crept into the garden in the dark. She was determined to bury her beloved dog herself, with no one watching. It was to be a private, personal goodbye, just the two of them. And so, in the driving rain, she blistered her hands digging the deepest hole she could. When it came up to her waist, she lowered Sally into it.

She had dressed the Westie in her best tartan jacket, wrapped her in a clean towel, with her favourite chewing sticks and a love note, and tied it all up with ribbons. Then, consumed with grief, she filled in the hole and collapsed. It was like this that her parents had found her.

For two weeks she had been gravely ill in hospital. Now the worst was over and she had been home for five days, but she would not eat and refused to get out of bed. She didn't want to see anyone.

Lil's parents were beside themselves with worry, so they hoped Cherry's plan today would work.

'Go away,' Lil told her.

Cherry sat on the bed.

'I got no time for wallowers,' she said bluntly. 'Self-pity is so ugly. Thought you was better than that.'

'Leave me alone.'

'Lords' sakes, you're stick-thin. That reminds me, the bones have all been re-interred and the rest of the town is back to normal – whatever that means. Anyway, we had us a huge meeting, strictly residents only. Boy, I told them a few home truths they won't never forget and finally outed myself as 'witch in residence'. That caused a few wet seats I can tell you. Well, we decided unanimously to put a lid on the whole Annie business. We gotta keep all that amongst ourselves. No one outside Whitby is ever gonna know. Who'd believe it anyways? They'd think the place was nuts. How's that for a mass conspiracy? The entire town is now guardin' this humungous secret. Pretty cool, huh?'

'I don't care.'

'Sure you do. And I read me some more of my predecessor's books. Remember how Annie was hanged and thrown into a cesspit? Well, seems the family of aufwaders she loved so much forgave her. They fished out her body, washed it, covered it in flowers, sang their sad songs over it and buried her on the cliff above their tunnels. After what she did to them, ain't that amazin'? If they can forgive that, isn't it time you forgave yourself? It wasn't your fault, babe.'

Lil turned over.

'Yes it was!' she said and Cherry saw that she was clutching Sally's fleecy blanket.

'Let me show you somethin',' Cherry said, rooting in her Mary Quant bag. 'I was gonna save this for when you was better, but what the heck.'

She brought out a large reproduction of a sepia photograph. It was one of hundreds taken by Frank Meadow Sutcliffe of Victorian Whitby. They were popular with the tourists, and many Whitby families, including the Wilsons and the Thistlewoods, had them on their walls because the people in them were ancestors.

The one she showed to Lil was of a group of elderly, wizened women sitting in the sun, mending fishing nets. Lil didn't bother looking at it. She'd seen them a million times and they all seemed the same.

Cherry waved it in her face.

'Look at it,' she told her. 'See this serious-faced gal stood behind them? Remind you of someone?'

Lil glanced at it just to shut her up. Then stared more closely.

'She . . . she looks like me,' she said in surprise. 'Must be a great-great-great-great-grandmother or something.'

Cherry sucked her teeth and shook her head. 'That's what I thought at first,' she said. 'Then I had a real close squint at it.'

Curious, Lil sat up and took the print from her. The resemblance was uncanny. Cherry took a magnifying glass out of her bag and passed it over.

'Fasten your seat belt, kid. Take a good look at what she's wearin' on that shawl.'

Lil moved the lens over the image. In spite of Cherry's words, she wasn't prepared for the shock it revealed.

'I can't believe it!' she gasped.

'You better start.'

The girl stared more closely. There was no doubt about it. There, pinned to the shawl, was one of her own home-made badges.

'How did she get that?'

'Don't be dumb, kid. She *is* you!'

'But . . . that's not possible.'

'You're still talkin' about possible and impossible? Really? Blinkers!'

'These photographs were taken over a hundred years ago.'

'And you was there. Ooooh, ain't that a puzzler? I have no idea how you managed that one, or are *gonna* manage it, I should say. Just don't let the guild of time witches find out; you don't wanna mess with those buzzkills. So you'd better stop feelin' sorry for yourself and get some fresh air inside you. Stinks of feet and puke and pre-teen angst in here.'

Lil peered through the magnifying glass to detect any sign of fakery, but the photograph looked totally genuine. She reached for the fleece at her side and stroked it.

'What you doin'?' Cherry asked.

'I pretend it's Sal,' the girl said sorrowfully.

'What?'

'Her old blanket.'

'This thing?'

Cherry held up the fleece. Lil didn't understand; if Cherry had it, then what was she stroking? Her heart beat faster. There was no mistaking that soft, silky fur. Then there was a movement and a wet nose pushed into the cup of her hand.

'Sal?' she murmured faintly.

A much-missed gentle tongue licked her palm.

'Sally!' she cried.

But, when she looked, there was nothing there.

'Well now!' Cherry exclaimed with an amused chuckle. 'Looks like Annie left you a partin' gift, sweetheart. She's taken away all the chains and padlocks you spent your life puttin' round your special talents. She might even have passed on some of her own skills. Welcome to the sisterhood. Lilith Wilson, you're a bona-fide witch.'

Lil burst into tears, but now she was laughing too.

Cherry rose and called Lil's father into the room.

'She's ready,' she said.

'What's happening?' the girl asked, blowing her nose.

'The town's cooked up somethin' special for you,' Cherry told her. 'It was my job to come get ya.'

'But I look a wreck! And I don't think I'm strong enough to walk yet.'

'You look beautiful,' her father said as he lifted her from the bed. 'And I'm going to carry you all the way.'

'Where's Mum?'

'She's waiting for us.'

Carrying his daughter from the bedroom, he gave Cherry a grateful smile.

Hearing them go down the stairs, Cherry wagged a finger at the empty spot on the bed where the Westie's ghost had fleetingly appeared.

'Don't you keep her awake at night,' she warned. 'That kid needs to get her strength back. She can't be playin' with you at all hours. There are tough times ahead. There's a lot I didn't tell her. Let her enjoy today; plenty of time to be scared later. The Lords of the Deep and Dark can't be thwarted so easy. She's gonna have to know all about them. She's got their attention – big time.'

When Mr Wilson emerged from the cottage with Lil in his arms, a great cheer went up. Lil was startled to see the street lined with people. All the neighbours were out to greet her. As Mr Wilson walked by, they clapped and wished her well.

The applause followed them down the street and the crowds along the way increased in number.

'Where are we going?' Lil asked.

'You'll see.'

By the time they reached the 199 steps, the street was thick with people and the cheering was tumultuous.

Lil gazed up at the steps; they too were crowded and everyone was smiling and waving at her.

Only one face in that throng was sullen. Tracy Evans watched Lil go by and her mouth twisted in a sneer as she took a photo of the nauseating scene to send to her beloved. The phone in her hand was crusty with dried blood and most of her fingers were bound in plasters. Another plaster would be needed later. Tracy despised the sickening adulation the Wilson girl was receiving, but she clung to the certainty that her gorgeous Dark would be with her soon. He had told her he'd been granted a second chance and just thinking about that sent Tracy's heart racing. Not long now . . .

With his daughter still in his arms, Mr Wilson climbed the steps. Lil felt like she was floating in a dream. Her head resting on his shoulder, she looked back at the town. Whitby had never looked more lovely. The sun was sparkling over the sea, fishing boats were bobbing in the harbour, the sky was deep blue and kipper smoke wafted across the cliff. Hundreds of beaming faces were thanking her for saving them and she murmured back politely. Some pressed bunches of flowers into her hands and soon she was decked out in blooms.

'It's all for you, Lil,' Mr Wilson said, bursting with pride. 'But you haven't seen the best part yet.'

Turning her head, Lil saw her mother standing at the top of the steps, with her arms extended in welcome. At her side was Verne.

'Put me down now, Dad,' she said. 'I can manage the last bit.'

Still clutching his hand, she reached the top, where another large crowd was gathered to greet her.

'Hello, darling,' her mother said, stroking her hair. 'This is Whitby's present to you.'

'What is?' Lil asked, confused.

'Everyone's taken part. Absolutely everyone. The whole town.'

There was a call for three cheers. As the jubilant hoorays rang across the cliff, the crowds parted and Lil finally saw what the people of Whitby had done for her.

The ancient graveyard was a mass of colour. Every single headstone, as far as the eye could see, was covered in a brightly knitted grave cosy. Even the Caedmon Cross was wrapped in a huge, gaudily striped scarf.

'It's for the Goth Weekend,' Mrs Wilson told her. 'Cherry told us you were behind those lovely decorations and what you'd been planning. From now on we're going to do this every year. It'll be a new tradition. Everyone loves it. And I love you.'

Lil didn't know what to say. Was there ever a more perfect day? Her eyes prickled again and then her legs felt weak and she reached for her father, but it was Verne who steadied her.

'Why haven't you been answering my texts?' he asked. 'It's all very well you having the mulligrubs, but what are we going to do about it?'

'Do about what?'

Verne pulled his rucksack open and Lil looked inside. A golden light shone up into her face.

'The Nimius!' she breathed in wonder.

'Ssshhh!' he told her, closing the bag hastily. 'No one knows I've still got it!'

Don't miss

THE DEVIL'S PAINTBOX

Coming soon